Dare to Dance

Dare to Dance

P. DIANE TRUSWELL
& MARY L. KLING

To order additional copies of this book, contact:
Xlibris Corporation
1-888-795-4274
www.Xlibris.com
Orders@Xlibris.com
42042

For Brad, Byron, Emily, Erica, and Hallie

Dance
feel the music
move to the beat
faster ever faster
to the rhythm of waves
under luminescent stars
Dance

Dare to Dance
until your feet tire
your shoes are worn
the night is over
the music stops
Dance

Dare to Dance
if you lose one dream
seek another
have faith that you will find
a way to move on
Dance

Dance
there is no tomorrow
all you have is now
Dance yes
Dance yes
Dare to dance.

CHAPTER 1

A bitter January wind swept down the snowless Connecticut street. As Karen turned into her driveway, the headlights of her BMW reflected no sign of life, not even the neighbor's ever-present cat. Only the dormant rose bushes greeted her, frozen sentries in a barren yard.

"Dark already," she mumbled as she trudged into the kitchen, balancing a stack of student notebooks and a carton of Chinese food. She dumped her armload on the counter, tossed her hooded parka over a chair, and snapped on the light. A glance at the clock told her it was 6:12 p.m. Why didn't the school board just put a cot in her classroom?

Grabbing her food and a fork, she headed for the family room, switched on a lamp, and looked around for the TV remote. And that's when she saw him, out of the corner of her eye.

She whirled around, hands flying to her face as Kung Pao chicken and egg roll with plum sauce fell, spattering red streaks across the plush ivory carpet. He was gone. He'd vanished again, leaving her with a mess.

"Just like you did when you were alive, you bastard!" Karen dropped to her knees, intending to salvage her dinner. Instead, she collapsed completely and began to pound the floor with her fists. "I hate you, Ari, I hate you," she screamed through angry tears. "Why can't you leave me alone?"

Spent, she lay facedown on the carpet, aware of the silence that pervaded her world. She could scream, but no one would hear. No one cared. Everyone avoided her now. Her friends, her coworkers, and her kids were all tired of her problems.

At least her kids hadn't witnessed this scene. Drew would be shocked. Mothers were supposed to nurture and protect, not screech and thrash around on the floor. Drew, who had such a strong sense of how the world should be. He'd be in for a surprise when he graduated from college in June.

Karen turned her head to study her children's portraits on the wall. Drew had inherited Karen's dark, curly hair and pale, smooth complexion. He'd grown into a handsome young man, but he was quiet. Too quiet. It might do him good if he yelled once in a while.

Her eyes shifted to the image of Drew's red-headed sister. Jocelyn would have no trouble hollering. She'd been exercising her vocal chords at full throttle since birth. Everyone within earshot always knew what Jocelyn thought, whether they wanted to or not. Jocelyn would have told her to get a grip, pick her ass up off the floor, and do it quickly. Jocelyn had never been known for patience.

Karen sat up to survey the mess on the carpet. How would she ever get the stain out, or the pungent vinegar smell? She'd have to call a professional.

Ha, a professional, she thought. The one person who might have applauded her performance came to mind. Margaret. Did a paid therapist count? Sure, Margaret encouraged her to get the feelings out, but Karen sensed the woman was less than absorbed with her words. Margaret always knew to the precise second when their fifty-minute session was up. The only person who encouraged her to speak these days charged her for the privilege.

On her knees, she tried to scoop the greasy blobs of food back into the carton with her fork, but the peanuts from the Kung Pao chicken resisted. She had no choice but to pick up the tacky morsels, one at a time, with her fingers. Karen gritted her teeth, hating the feel of anything sticky. Persnickety, Ari always said. Ari again, damn it. He'd been dead two years and three months. Why did he have to invade her every thought?

Come to think of it, he even invaded her non-thoughts. She didn't have anything in her mind when he appeared tonight. It was always the same, a flash and then gone. By now, she should be used to it. Since the day she'd come home from the funeral, it had happened at least once a week.

The funeral. What a farce. Everyone sitting in the pews knew the story. Karen's face felt hot now at the thought of it. Her family trying to hold their heads high at the front of the church while that journalist jerk, Adrian, sat in the back. Afterward, in the line, most people could barely look her in the eye. But that nervy bastard had fixed his intense blue eyes right on her until she was the one who had to look down, forced to stare at his fancy leather shoes.

CHAPTER 2

*S*hoes. *She's seven years old, surrounded by presents on Christmas morning. An only child, all the presents under the fragrant fir are hers. But the gift she wants most she knows she'll never receive. It is her secret wish, never to be shared. If only her mother and dad would give her a brother or sister.*

Her mother beams and hands her a silver box with a giant red bow. She takes it from her mother's hands. Her father watches.

Silent, she removes the bow then the tape. The paper rustles as she slips off the wrapping intact, careful even then. She opens the box. It is a pair of white leather ballet slippers. Dazzling shoes. She runs her hand over their smooth, soft surface. They are the most beautiful shoes she has ever seen.

She takes them from the box, smells their newness, clutches them to her heart. Could it be possible; could this mean ballet lessons? Her mother says yes. Her father nods.

Happy. At seven years old, she loves to dance. She puts on her new shoes and is a dancer. The living room is her stage, her parents the audience. She dances the dance of the Sugar Plum Fairy. She hears the music in her mind. Her mother and father beam at her in her new shoes.

CHAPTER 3

In a two-bedroom student apartment eighty miles from his childhood home, Drew watched the fish in the tank on the Formica counter. From the kitchen, Drew could see his roommate Colin in the living room plopped in the middle of one of the two well-worn couches, surrounded by a mountain of books. The entire apartment was carpeted in a tired beige, the same color as the furniture. The only color in the room came from the three Toulouse-Lautrec Moulin Rouge posters hanging on the smudged off-white walls.

This semester, Colin had been so engrossed with his studies that he seldom remembered to feed his fish. Drew picked up the container of fish flakes and sprinkled a pinch into the water for the three varieties of danios, seven neon tetras, and the spotted corydora. Next to the ten-gallon tank was a smaller one for Drew's favorite, the royal blue betta. They'd removed the betta from the larger community because the other fish liked to chew its beautiful tail. Drew put a miniscule amount in the betta's tank as well.

Colin tended to dump in a large amount of food when he thought of it, but Drew preferred to do smaller feedings several times a day. He'd sense the eyes of the fish as they lined up on his side of the tank when he entered the kitchen. They seemed to recognize him and know he wouldn't forget them.

Good thing Colin had needed a roommate three years ago; otherwise, Drew guessed he'd be living alone somewhere or in a dorm with freshmen.

Drew set the fish food aside. Time to get to work. He'd hardly cracked a book since the semester started, and now midterms loomed.

This would be his last semester at the University of Hartford if he was lucky. He glanced at the fish again. Freedom—that's what he wanted. He'd move far from Hartford, far from Stamford and his mother. Probably he should move far from his sister in New York City too. As far from his father's world as he could.

Drew clenched his teeth. Here he was, following in his dad's footsteps, majoring in economics and finance. Even attending the same school. What an idiotic thing to do. He was nothing like his stockbroker dad. But this decision had been made long before his dad got cancer, long before he dropped his bombshell.

His dad. Smart. Mr. Popularity everywhere he went, not a shadow in the background. Drew rested his forefinger lightly on the glass of the betta's bowl.

Colin's gruff voice interrupted his thoughts. "Drew, stop fussing with the fish. You're pissing me off. I thought you were going to study."

"Yeah, yeah. I'm getting to it. Give me a break." Drew pulled a can of Mountain Dew from the refrigerator. On the way to his threadbare spot on the other sofa, he collected his advanced economics book from the cluttered dining room table, resisting the impulse to pick up his sketchbook.

He'd read only half a page when the phone rang. No point jumping up. The calls were always for Colin.

"Yeah?" Colin barked into the phone. Seconds later, his voice changed to the syrupy polite tone he reserved for parents and professors. "Oh, hello, Mrs. Antilla." A forced smile spread over his face. "I'm fine, thank you. Yes, he's here. Drew, it's your mother."

Drew sucked in a deep breath and let it out slowly as Colin tossed him the cordless phone. He abandoned his econ book and sauntered to the dining room table to take a seat.

"Hi, Mom." He knew his voice lacked enthusiasm, but it was the best he could do.

"Hi, sweetheart. Haven't talked with you in a while. Thought I'd call before you were up to your ears in books. I know it's almost time for midterms."

"You're right, it is." Drew opened his sketchbook.

"Just a few more months and a few more tests, and you'll be out of school."

"Yup, I know," Drew picked up a pencil and turned to the drawing he had begun of a white-tailed doe. He'd spotted her yesterday while walking on the parkway, and their eyes had locked for a long moment.

"I'm sure you're looking forward to that. I remember how it was when I was in school. Not that the working world is always enjoyable. For example, would you believe Mr. McKinley suggested I teach first-year algebra next year? After I've taught advanced algebra and calculus for all these years, I feel like I'm about to be demoted."

Drew's pencil outlined the doe's staring, frightened eyes. "Sorry, Mom. I know you enjoy working with advanced students."

"Intro classes are always draining. The kids aren't excited about learning like they are in advanced math. Although this year, my algebra II class is a pain, as well."

"That's too bad." His pencil moved to the doe's high pointed ears.

"But enough about me. How are you doing?" his mother asked.

Drew put his pencil down and closed the sketchbook. "Nothing new here. Just studying for midterms, like you said. I've got some rough ones."

"Oh, really? I'm sure you'll do fine, but make sure you're eating well and getting enough sleep. Are you sleeping okay?"

"Yup, will do. How about you, Mom? How have you been doing?"

"Well, now that you mention it, I haven't been sleeping well again. It's hard to go to work in a lion's den every day without a good night's sleep."

"Maybe you should see your doctor." Drew pursed his lips and stared at a crack in the ceiling. He remembered the sleeping pills the doctor had prescribed for them both after his dad died.

"It's just having too much on my mind. What could a doctor do about what's happened in our family?"

Drew knew the direction the conversation would take now. It never changed. No matter how it started, eventually it came back to the same topic. He thought about the deer bounding back into the woods, its white tail rising up like a flag.

"I'm sorry you're not sleeping well, but I've really got to study, Mom."

There was a short silence. "I guess I'm bothering you."

"No," Drew lied, tapping his pencil on the closed sketchbook. "It's just that I've got to study."

His mother sighed. "Go back to your books. Hope you'll be able to come home soon. I'd like an excuse to bake something."

Drew felt guilty for letting his impatience show. "Glad you called," he said gently. "I'll be home the weekend after midterms. Maybe Jocelyn can get off work."

"I'll call her. And don't worry about me. I'm doing okay."

"Good, Mom. Talk to you soon. I'll call. Promise." Drew put the receiver down and exhaled in relief.

CHAPTER 4

The classroom always smelled stale when Karen walked in after a weekend. The first thing she did was open the one small window to let in fresh air, even in the throes of winter, like now.

She usually came early to organize her desk, review her lessons, and enjoy a final cup of her favorite hazelnut-flavored coffee before the students arrived.

First-hour calculus was her favorite class this year. They were delightful students, most of them college bound. She enjoyed the challenge of working with questioning minds, and today her students didn't disappoint.

Fourth-hour advanced algebra was a different story. When Karen turned to write an equation on the board, the class erupted in laughter. She turned around to see what was happening and saw nothing. She ignored it and began to write another equation. More laughter. She figured someone was probably making faces or gesturing behind her back. She continued to ignore it.

When the class burst into laughter a third time, Karen had to say something. "Okay, what's causing the commotion?"

Silence. Determined to continue the lesson, she turned back to the chalkboard. This time her chalk broke, making a squealing sound, and the class guffawed again. She picked up another piece of chalk and kept writing without turning around.

Suddenly pencils clattered to the gray-tiled floor like pick-up sticks. She turned to face her class. Twenty-four straight-faced students scuffled to retrieve the pencils.

Karen glared. "What's the problem here?"

Twenty-three blank faces stared straight ahead. Only Roger Delacroix smirked. Blonde, athletic, and popular, he seemed to enjoy the role of class clown. Years ago, she'd learned the most obnoxious students could turn out to be scholars.

"What do you know about this, Roger?"

"Why would I know anything?" Roger feigned surprise. "I'm just trying to learn."

Pencils dropped to the floor once more. Again, expressionless students clamored to pick them up.

"See, it isn't me," said Roger, his blue eyes wide with innocence. "My pencil is still on my desk."

Karen was furious. She wanted to teach her lesson. "If we can't get through class today without disruption, perhaps we'll have class during the lunch hour."

"Oh, you can't do that, Mrs. Antilla," Kevin Rush, Roger's friend, blurted from the back of the room. "It's a law. We get our lunch break."

Karen could feel her face turning red. What he said was true. She shouldn't have made the threat. The blare of the electronic bell signaled the end of class. Thank God.

While the students marched out of the room, Karen's eyes smarted. The lesson would have to be repeated tomorrow, and she was already behind schedule.

Grateful for her lunch hour, Karen closed the classroom door so she could eat and correct papers in peace. She couldn't choke down more than a few bites of her ham-and-cheese sandwich.

She jumped when she heard the click of the door opening. Mr. McKinley stepped into the room. "Karen, sorry to bother you. Do you have a moment?" A former army major, his countenance, was all business. At six foot four, the principal towered over her in his impeccable suit and tie.

Karen made a feeble attempt to smile, placing her red pen on the desk. "Sure, John. I'm correcting papers, but they can wait. Not enough hours in the day."

The smell of English Leather aftershave wafted over her. He turned a student desk around to face her, squeezing himself into the seat. "Roger Delacroix stopped to visit me a few minutes ago on his way to lunch." He tapped a well-manicured finger on the desk.

Karen straightened in her chair. "Oh?"

"He told me you accused him of disrupting class this morning. Is that true?"

She felt her face flush. She should have known Roger would try to make trouble for her. "Every time I turned to write on the chalkboard, the class broke into chaos. All I did was ask Roger if he knew anything about it."

Mr. McKinley leaned back and folded his arms across his chest. "Roger felt accused. He told me you're always singling him out for ridicule."

"That's not true." Karen's face reddened even more. "He's caused trouble in my class in the past. Admittedly, he was the first student who came to mind, and he looked guilty. It might've been someone else. But, to be honest, I don't think so."

The principal continued, "Roger said you lost control of the class, and you threatened to take away their lunch hour. Is that true?"

"I had to say something," she said, feeling backed into a corner. "I just couldn't let it go. I did not lose control."

He shook his head. "Karen, you've got to get a grip. High school students will test you. This isn't the first time this year a student has told me you've had trouble with classroom management."

"John, you know I have a couple of rough classes," she said, thinking he'd assigned them to her on purpose.

"Yes, but the parents in this community expect their teachers to be able to cope. They don't look with favor upon disorder or reports of teachers harassing students."

Karen knew she couldn't argue. "I'm sorry, John."

Mr. McKinley stood, indicating he was about to leave. "I know you've had a difficult few years. I've tried to be understanding, but I have to think about what's good for the students. We can't let teachers' personal problems interfere. Next year, as we've talked about before, I think you'll be happier with more first-year algebra and perhaps a geometry class. Even a general math. Less pressure."

Karen felt a lump in her throat. "Mr. McKinley, my personal problems are behind me. My priority is doing my job well. I arrive early and never leave before five o'clock at night. Ask anyone in the math department."

McKinley returned the student desk to its position. "I know you work hard. But I don't like to hear student or parent complaints. We'll talk again. I'll let you get back to your lunch now."

Karen studied his back as he left then walked to the window to open it even wider in an effort to rid the room of the smell of his aftershave.

* * *

After the final bell, Karen walked across the hall to the room of the only coworker she'd call a friend. Siri and she seldom socialized outside school, but they were close to the same age and had been working together for fifteen years.

"What a day. I'm perfectly exhausted." Karen flopped into a student desk. "I've got to get off my feet."

Siri turned from the chalkboard. At five foot ten inches, she was somewhat of a contrast to five-foot-six Karen with her willowy figure and classically styled dark-blond hair pulled back softly from her face. "Yes, these winter days are rough," she replied. She stopped writing and sat at her desk so they could talk. "What's up?"

"Good old parent-pleasing McKinley descended upon me at noon. Roger Delacroix complained that I accused him of something he didn't do, but I know he did it. McKinley criticized my classroom management. Can you imagine?"

"What a jackass." Siri shook her head sympathetically.

"Who? McKinley or Roger?"

"Both of them."

Karen and Siri laughed then Karen told the whole story.

"No wonder you're exhausted," said Siri. "Hard enough to do your job without John ruining a perfectly good noon hour."

"It sure threw me for a loop. Thanks for listening. I know you're busy too. I'd better get back to work." Karen rose to leave.

Siri stood. "Don't let McKinley get you down with his we-must-please-the-parents bull. We've all danced to that tune."

Siri's words echoed through her mind as Karen returned to her classroom. *Danced to that tune.*

CHAPTER 5

*D*ancing. *She feels his glance from across the room. The band begins to play. The tall handsome auburn-haired man must be looking at someone else. But no, she smiles at him, and he smiles back. It is her.*

He approaches, asks her to dance. A fast dance with a strong beat. Yes, she says, she'd like that. He takes her hand and guides her to the dance floor. He is a superior dancer. So is she. They glide gracefully, as if they'd danced together for years.

He says he noticed her; something told him she was a good dancer. His rich mellow voice is confident. His soft green shirt smells like laundry fresh from the line. He tells her his name is Ari, Ari Antilla.

She says she's Karen, Karen Rose Whittaker, as she floats in his strong arms. He says she is as beautiful as her name. They continue to dance. With him, she is not shy. When he asks if he can see her again, she says yes. Oh yes.

CHAPTER 6

The ten-year-old blue Mustang pulled into the Stamford driveway. As Drew climbed out, a pale orange-striped cat approached.

"Igor," Drew said as he knelt to pet his familiar friend. "What's up, old fellow? What are you doing out on a snowy night?"

The cat began to purr when Drew massaged behind his ears. "I can always count on you being here." As Drew stood, he nudged Igor toward the Wilsons' house next door. "Better get on home now. It's cold."

Igor meowed and moseyed off.

At the door, Drew hesitated. He fingered the house key on his key chain. He hadn't been home since Christmas. It didn't feel right to just walk in. He rang the bell instead.

Jocelyn opened the door, all smiles, in her usual worn jeans and oversized T-shirt. He was grateful to see his sister. Sometimes it was hard to be the sole recipient of his mother's anguish.

"Hey, Drew." Jocelyn pulled him close and squeezed him hard. He could feel the warmth emanating from her small frame. Drew tried to relax, but his arms felt as stiff as icicles.

"You beat me home," he offered.

She tucked a lock of rust-colored hair behind her ear. "Mom picked me up at the train station an hour ago. I'm off until Sunday night. I told my boss it was an important family occasion." She winked.

His mother entered the foyer, smiling. She looked comfortable in her rose-colored velour jogging suit. "Oh, you're here. Welcome home, sweetheart." She hugged him tightly.

"Hi, Mom, nice to be home. What's that I smell? Chocolate?"

"Yes, I baked a cake. Why don't you put your bag in your room, dear, while I put the coffee on. We'll eat in the living room."

Jocelyn and Drew exchanged glances. The family seldom gathered in the formal living room, meticulously decorated in Louis XV style. The casually furnished family room was more comfortable.

"I'm looking forward to a nice weekend," Karen continued. "A piece of cake won't interfere with anyone's diet, will it?"

Drew retrieved his duffle bag from his car and took it upstairs to his old bedroom. He tossed the bag on the bed, noting his room still looked the same as it had in his high school years. Model airplanes on the shelf, his old sketchbooks stacked on the desk, the telescope in the corner. Drew looked up at the ceiling fan, his rescue helicopter. He grinned as he flipped the switch to turn it on. Drew Antilla, jungle explorer, liberator, and avenger in Chopper X reporting.

How long ago those days seemed.

*   *   *

When Drew returned to the living room, Karen was cutting the cake and placing it onto his favorite plates, the ones with the little fish. He took a seat in one of the curvy rococo chairs. He wasn't particularly hungry, but that didn't matter. The cake would be served. The cake would be eaten.

"Drew, here's a big piece for you. I know chocolate's your favorite. Jocelyn, here's yours. Oh, wait, I forgot the coffee." Karen scurried off to the kitchen.

Drew rolled his eyes, as he and Jocelyn sat with their plates.

Jocelyn snickered. "Nothing's changed since last time we were home, bro. Nothing." She took a small bite of the cake. "Ugh, I can't eat this. Too sweet." She pushed the plate into the middle of the ornate curvy-legged table.

Karen returned with the coffee. Drew divided his cake into sections with his fork. *Easier to eat,* he thought.

His mother inquired about their health, speculated about the weather, and updated them on the status of the neighborhood. Apparently, Igor had disappeared for a couple of days but had eventually been found trapped in the garage of the couple across the street when they had returned from a weekend jaunt. To the relief of the neighborhood, he was once again ambling in and out of his residence via his usual route, the cat door.

"The adventures of Igor continue," Jocelyn joked, speculating that Igor must be on about his eighth life by now.

Drew enjoyed Jocelyn's hearty laugh and delighted in his mother's animated storytelling ability, something she had almost lost of late. They continued to chat lightheartedly about Jocelyn's job and Drew's classes, but then his mother turned to the subject of Jocelyn's departure from college.

"Jocelyn," Karen said, pouring coffee into a mug, "I wish you'd go back. You were always such a good student in high school." Karen turned to Drew. "Don't you think she should go back to school?"

"That's her decision," Drew mumbled, gulping down a second helping of cake. The chocolate cream cheese frosting was too good to resist.

Karen frowned and turned back to Jocelyn. "You'll never make enough money as a waitress, honey. What's the future in a job like that?"

No one answered. Put off only briefly by the silence, Karen helped herself to a second serving of cake and continued. "I guess we should talk about other things." She turned to Drew. "How were your midterms?"

Drew shrugged. "Okay, I guess. I'll have to wait and see."

"Your father should be here. He's the one who had a business head, the one who would've been able to tell you where to apply for jobs." Karen set her plate on the marble-topped coffee table and took a sip of coffee.

"I can handle it, Mom. I'm going to a job fair next month. That'll help." He hoped she'd get off the subject.

"It's hard living in this house." Karen took a deep breath. "I still think it was Adrian's fault. If it hadn't been for Adrian . . ."

Drew's stomach churned. He gave up any thought of finishing the cake. His mother was starting. He looked at Jocelyn. Her face was beginning to color.

Jocelyn spoke, her voice shaking, "Mom, that's not true. You can't blame everything on him."

Karen set her china cup down. "Not true? Of course, it's true. That man ruined my life, and don't pretend it didn't affect you both too. He destroyed everything I believed in, he destroyed our family."

Jocelyn exploded. "Damn it, Mother, how can you say that? You don't know Adrian!"

"Keep your voice down," scolded Karen. "I don't know what kind of spell that man had over your father, but it was evil, and I won't accept any of this other garbage everyone tries to hand me."

"Mom, Dad was gay. Period."

"Yes, and he was a liar too," Karen said, bursting into tears.

His sister's color deepened. Ever since she was a kid, Drew could gauge his sister's mood by her color. Right now, she was clearly furious.

He tried to speak, but his mouth was too dry. He swallowed and cleared his throat. "Mom, Jocelyn, calm down. This is old stuff. Do we need to bring this up over and over again?"

Neither Karen nor Jocelyn appeared to hear him.

"Yes, I know. I've heard the theories. No one would choose to be gay." Karen glared at Jocelyn. "I certainly didn't choose to be humiliated and lied to, either. I had no choice in the matter, and neither did you. How either of you can defend your father is beyond me."

"Dad turning out to be gay didn't change who he was." Angry tears filled Jocelyn's eyes. "He was a terrific father, and I wish every day I could have him back. It kills me, Mom, when you trash Dad."

Drew squinted. His eyes hurt. He opened his mouth to speak again, but nothing would come. His hands were clammy.

His mother's demeanor softened a bit. "Your father deceived me, but that damned Adrian took him away from us. He knew Ari was married. He knew we were a family. Adrian should have left your dad alone."

Jocelyn's voice rose again, her face almost purple. "Mom, you're just never going to get it, are you? Dad was fucking gay, and so am I!" She leaped to her feet, hands on her hips. "What do you think of that?"

Karen paled and leaned back. One hand clutched the gilt-painted arm of the satin sofa, and the other covered her mouth.

Drew closed his eyes. No. Not Jocelyn too. In the distance, he could hear a familiar whirring sound. His ceiling fan. He'd forgotten to turn it off.

"But you can't . . . but you don't . . . ," Karen stammered. "Jocelyn, it can't be. You're hysterical. You don't know what you're saying." Flustered, Karen stood and looked around. "I think we need some air in here. Drew, open a window." She picked up a magazine and fanned her face.

Drew opened his eyes, feeling like a robot. He complied with his mother's wish. All three were standing, now, in the middle of the room. Jocelyn glowered. Karen continued to fan herself. Drew's stomach cramped.

No one spoke for a long minute. Finally, Karen sat down. "That's better. We needed fresh air. Jocelyn, Drew, sit down please."

They did as she asked, but Jocelyn was obviously still irate.

"Now, Jocelyn, I know how quickly you decide things. Too quickly. I seriously doubt—"

Jocelyn interrupted. "I know what I'm talking about." Her voice had a quiet, icy edge. "This is nothing I decided last week. I've known I was gay since I was eight years old."

"Nonsense. You can't possibly know until . . . ," Karen's voice trailed off.

"Until I fuck someone, Mom?" Jocelyn threw her head back and let out a mirthless laugh. "Fear not, I already have. And, yup, I even did it with a guy once, and you know what? There was no comparison."

"Jocelyn, your language! And you're sitting there telling me you've had sex with a woman?"

"Women, Mom, as in more than one. In fact, I'm seeing one right now. She's definitely a woman, and we've definitely had sex."

Drew gripped the arms of the chair while he listened to his sister and his mother. He felt detached, invisible, an actor forced to watch a movie in which he had no part.

"Had sex? Where?" asked his mother. "Not in the family apartment! My father, may he rest in peace, would be beside himself if he knew that was going on in the apartment he bought your father and me. Please tell me you haven't been seeing this woman there!"

"Get a grip, Mother. What in hell does it matter where I have sex? I'm a dyke. Get that through your head."

Karen turned white. Drew feared she might faint.

"I can't take this, Jocelyn. How could you do this to me?"

Jocelyn threw a glance in Drew's direction. "Here we go again. Same old, same old." She looked back at her mother. "Mom, no one is doing anything to you. I'm simply trying to live my life in some kind of honest fashion, and that's what Dad was trying to do, too."

Karen's hands shook. "Whatever you do in your life, with women, I don't want to see. I don't like your news, and I don't ever, and I do mean ever, want you to bring a woman to this house."

"Fine." Jocelyn stood. "If you can't accept who I am, or whom I might love, I guess there's no point in hanging around. I'll just get my bag, and I'm out of here. Have a nice life, Mom." Jocelyn started up the stairs.

"Wait . . ." Drew couldn't let this happen. "Jocelyn, Mom . . ."

"Don't worry, Drew. She'll be back," Karen scoffed, not taking her eyes off Jocelyn on the stairs. "Without her grandparents' trust money and the family apartment, your sister couldn't exist. She'll talk to me all right. She'll have to, in order to maintain her standard of living."

"Mother, you are a complete bitch." Jocelyn tossed over her shoulder. "Drew, if you want to help, you can drive me to the train station."

Drew glanced at his mother.

"Go ahead," Karen said with a shrug.

*   *   *

Ten minutes later, Drew and Jocelyn were in the car on the way to the station.

"Sorry, bro, I couldn't help it."

Drew winced. "Yeah, I know. You've always had to speak your mind. Wish you hadn't upset her, though. She's hard enough to deal with when she doesn't have ammunition."

"Well, until she starts facing the truth of how things were instead of how she wishes they'd been, she's going to stay stuck right where she is. Personally, I can't deal with it. I'm sorry."

"Yeah," Drew repeated. "I understand."

Jocelyn studied his face. "Drew, did you know about me?"

"No, I didn't. That was a surprise. I just have to ask once, and I won't ask again. Are you sure?"

She reached over to touch the back of his hand. "I'm sure. Are you okay with it?"

"I don't know what I think sometimes. But it's okay. You're my kid sister, and I'll never turn my back on you, Josey." Drew hoped the nickname he'd given her when they were young would bring a smile to her face.

The corners of Jocelyn's mouth turned upward. "Thanks. Sorry, I sprang that on you."

They arrived at the station. Jocelyn squeezed Drew's hand and headed for the double doors. Drew watched as she disappeared into the building. He felt sorry for Jocelyn. He felt sorry for his mother. How he wished he could have done something besides just sit there.

CHAPTER 7

Jocelyn tried to submerge herself in the pajama feel of her forest-green flannel sheets, but nothing would allow her to forget the night before. There was no reason to get up since she wasn't in Stamford. She didn't need to be at work until late Sunday afternoon.

By ten o'clock, hunger forced her from bed. She pulled on a pair of jeans and a white Wagner College T-shirt and walked barefoot to the kitchen to see what she could scrounge. The black and white tiles chilled her feet. Her stomach rumbled.

"Darn," she cursed. The refrigerator was not promising: a case of beer, three cartons of yogurt, two apples, some wilted celery, and a mysterious Styrofoam container. When she lifted the lid, the pungent odor of garlic wafted out. *Oh yeah. Tuesday's shrimp scampi from the restaurant. Probably too old now.* She tossed the carton into the garbage and checked out the freezer: popsicles, stir-fried veggies, and a small box of Haagen-Dazs rocky road ice cream.

She slammed the freezer door closed, breaking the silence of the room. *Damn. Not a piece of bread in the house. Toast would have been good.* She settled for a blueberry yogurt, taking it with her to the living room.

Sitting cross-legged on the burgundy brocade sofa, she savored the sharp-sweet taste and wondered what she'd do with the afternoon. She put down her spoon and looked around for the phone. There it was, on the coffee table. Her fingers tapped the familiar numbers.

"Hi, Adrian. It's me, Jocelyn. Are you busy? No? Want to meet me in the park for a walk? It's not snowing, doesn't seem too cold. Good. Okay. What time? Eleven? See you then. Usual spot. Bye."

CHAPTER 8

Half-awake, Drew imagined he was in grade school again, looking around his room. His model airplanes rested on the shelves, all twenty-three of them. As a child, he'd spent hours building these models while other kids were shooting baskets or running to home plate. Never confident about his athletic ability, he'd tried to avoid the neighborhood games so he wouldn't make a fool of himself.

Jocelyn, on the other hand, always played outside with her friends. That is, until Dad introduced her to golf. Then she left her worn leather baseball glove and her regulation basketball behind in her closet, where they probably still could be found today.

Drew's eyes lingered on his sketchbooks on the desk. He loved to wander the woodlands and wetlands. There was always so much to observe: ferns and wildflowers, blue-winged warblers, foxes, raccoons and, once in a while, a wandering black bear.

"Drew, are you awake?" The sound of his mother's voice, raring to go, roused him from his early morning reverie.

"Be down in a minute, Mom." He pulled on a pair of jeans and a blue-and-white flannel shirt, aware of the chill of the February air. He'd agreed to come home for the weekend, so he was determined to stay. *Damn, why did Jocelyn have to get into it with Mom?*

"How about brunch at the Meadow Inn this morning?" Surprisingly, his mother's mood was upbeat. "I'd planned to take you and your sister," she added.

"Sure. Sounds good." He loved the big puffy Belgian waffles at the Meadow Inn. He could almost conjure up the sweet just-baked smell of them now. The restaurant had always been a family favorite for everyone, including Dad.

CHAPTER 9

Jocelyn hurried the five blocks from the Antilla apartment to Central Park's 86th Street entrance. Adrian would walk nine blocks from the other direction.

He was waiting on a bench when she arrived.

"Hey, Adrian."

"Hey," he replied, giving her a brief hug. "Glad you're here."

They began to walk, gloveless hands stuffed into winter parkas, taking their usual path toward the lake. Patches of snow covered the ground, but the walkway was clear. Although it hadn't snowed in two weeks, today the air had the crisp smell of winter.

"So what's up?" Adrian's intense blue eyes sparkled in the sunlight. "Haven't heard from you in a while."

Jocelyn swept her hair back from her face. "Saw Mom yesterday, in Stamford. The good news is I finally came out to her, like you said I should."

She glanced at Adrian. He looked surprised, but he didn't speak, apparently in anticipation of more to come. Adrian knew how to listen. Really listen.

Hearing the sound of heavy breathing behind her, she moved aside to let a fast-moving runner pass. "But the bad news is, I wasn't exactly polite."

Adrian frowned. They walked several paces before he spoke again. "How did she take it?"

Jocelyn scrutinized the icy waters of the lake. "Not well. I left before she could say much. I wasn't going to open my big mouth when I went there yesterday, but she started in about Dad again. And you."

"I'm sorry," said Adrian, shaking his head.

"I'm so damned tired of it. I snapped. I said, 'I'm a dyke, you're a judgmental bitch,' and I ran out of the house. Drew had to take me to the station."

Adrian stopped in the path. "Drew was there? What did he say?"

"Not much." She had stopped too. "He was sorry I'd upset Mom, but he's sick of her going on and on about the same stuff, like I am."

Adrian frowned as they resumed walking. "The news is out, at least," he said. "You can't expect her initial reaction to be complete acceptance. It's a shock, but your mom loves you. She'll come around once she has time to adjust."

"Not my mom! It's been two years, and how well has she adjusted to the truth about you and Dad? She sure as hell isn't over that."

"I know, but that's different. There are other issues. It's hard enough for her to adjust to your dad dying, not to mention me."

"But you've adjusted. You had the same loss."

Adrian's smile was sad, and his eyelids seemed to twitch a little. "Let's just say I'm surviving, Jocelyn. I have more good days than bad, but still, there are times when it's hard."

Jocelyn read the pain in his face. "I don't suppose it's ever occurred to Mom how hard it is for you."

Adrian returned to the original subject. "It might take some time, but I do believe she'll accept you. You're her daughter."

"Ha!" Jocelyn snorted. "She told me I'd better not darken her doorstep with my girlfriend."

Again, Adrian came to a halt in the pathway. "You have a girlfriend?"

"Well, no." Jocelyn blushed as she cleared her throat. "I exaggerated a bit. Told her I did. Said I'd slept with a bunch of women. I was pissed."

Adrian reached out to tousle Jocelyn's windblown hair even more than it already was. "You little brat," he chuckled, "you love to shock people. But your poor mom."

This time, Jocelyn was the one to start walking again, the heels of her boots making a clipped staccato sound as they struck the paved path. "Okay, so I don't have a girlfriend. But I might someday. The point is, Mom doesn't want to see me with a woman. Not only that, if she knew I'd never been with a woman, she wouldn't believe I'm a lesbian, and as you know, I don't have any doubt."

With a pensive look, Adrian patted her arm. "I know you don't."

CHAPTER 10

The attentive woman at the hostess station was the wife of the longtime owner. "Table for two?" Mrs. Martin asked, picking up two menus as she spoke.

"Yes, Eloise, could we have a booth, please?"

The hostess took a second look. "Why, Karen, I didn't recognize you. I haven't seen you in a long time. How are you?"

"Better some days than others." Karen's smile was strained.

"I remember when you used to come here with your husband. What a tragedy." Mrs. Martin shook her head sympathetically. "He was so young." She led them to a booth near the window.

Something about the way Mrs. Martin looked at his mother made Drew suspect she liked to gossip.

"Is this booth all right?"

"Yes, Eloise. Thanks."

As they settled, the hostess presented their menus with a flourish and retreated to her station. The smell of bacon wafted their direction from the nearby omelet station.

"Mom, I remember we all used to come here once in a while," said Drew in an attempt to make small talk.

"Yes, I'd hoped the three of us could enjoy it this morning." Karen took a sip of the ice water that was already on the table. "Drew, I'm sorry for what happened yesterday. I shouldn't have lost it like I did, and I wish your sister hadn't lost it too. I hope we can work it out."

Drew didn't know what to say, but he felt obligated to reply. "I'm sure it'll be okay, Mom."

With an elbow on the table, Karen lowered her head into the palm of her hand. "I must admit, I don't understand your sister. I couldn't sleep last night. This is so hard. First your father. Now Jocelyn. Running off as she did. Drew, you won't leave me, will you?"

Drew opened his menu, noticing the background noise of forks clinking against china. "No, of course not." He felt guilty as he remembered his post college plans.

"I have to talk to someone about these things," Karen said.

Drew nodded as the server appeared at the table.

Karen held out her closed menu. "We'll both have the brunch buffet, won't we, Drew?"

"Sure." Drew tried to sound enthusiastic. "I can hardly wait to dive into the waffles."

The server smiled. "Okay, help yourself when you're ready."

"Let's get some food, and we can continue our talk," said Karen. They walked through the brunch line and came back to the booth, plates heaped. Drew's waffles were buried in fresh sliced strawberries, a large dollop of whipped cream, and a generous sprinkling of walnuts. Karen had returned with two plates, one for her Spanish omelet and apple crepes, and a smaller plate for a blueberry muffin and a good-sized piece of coffee cake.

"Drew, I just have to know. Did you have any idea about Jocelyn? Do you really think she's gay?" Karen took a bite of her muffin.

"Mom, if she said so, then she is." He cut into a piece of waffle with his fork.

"She's always had such a temper."

Drew squirmed and put his fork down for a moment, fearing this might be one of the longest meals he'd ever eaten. "She's always had strong opinions, and so have you."

"It's so hard for me to deal with all this. Hard enough to find out that your dad had cancer. Then to find out he was gay. I still can't believe he didn't know before he married me."

Drew knew he should remain neutral, but he couldn't help himself. He glanced around and leaned into the table. "I can't either. Look at Jocelyn. She said she knew when she was eight."

Karen shook her head. "Somehow I think your dad's gayness must have influenced your sister. Or else she's saying these things just to upset me."

Drew frowned. "I don't think so."

"I just can't take one more thing," Karen said, shaking her head.

"I know it's hard."

Karen continued. "My whole world fell apart. Your father's death was bad enough, but how can I face people when they know he was with that man Adrian? Spending all those nights with him in our apartment in the city. And now Jocelyn, entertaining her women friends. What is it about that apartment? Oh god, I can't bear it." Karen put her head in her hands again.

"Yeah, Mom. I know." They'd had this conversation at least a dozen times in the past year, but nothing he said had ever had any impact.

"No one understands. We didn't have many common friends. Your dad worked in New York City, and—"

"Yes, I know." Drew knew what was coming next. "And he often stayed there on business overnight."

"Yes, and what business that was."

"You've got to get over it, Mom." Drew pushed his plate back from the edge of the table, no longer able to eat.

"I'm sorry Drew. I didn't mean to go on and on."

"That's okay." Drew placed his cutlery on the plate and tried to smile.

They sat in silence while Karen finished her pastry and accepted another cup of coffee from the waiter. "How about you? Have you been having any kind of fun? Dating at all?"

Drew fidgeted. As much as he didn't want to talk about his mother's problems, he wanted even less to talk about himself. "No, I haven't had time. Busy studying. It's been a tough semester. I'm glad this is the last."

"I wish you'd try to get out more. College is a good place to meet someone." Tears trickled down Karen's cheeks.

Drew could sense other patrons in the restaurant watching his mother. "Maybe we should go."

"You're right, of course. Not good to cry in public. And I wanted this to be such a pleasant meal." Karen dabbed at her eyes with a napkin.

CHAPTER 11

As he scanned the panorama of tall buildings visible through the bare trees, Adrian wondered what he should say to Jocelyn. He'd first met her at the hospital when Ari was dying. Although she'd given him a civil nod at the funeral, he'd never expected to become her mentor.

He remembered the first time she turned up on his doorstep, two months after Ari's death. He'd recognized her immediately when he opened the door. She'd glared at him with her arms crossed, almost challenging him to shut the door in her face. Instead, he'd invited her in.

At first, she'd just seemed curious about her father's lover. She wanted to know him, to understand what the attraction had been. She was still a student then at Wagner College on Staten Island. When she continued to drop in, he began to suspect there must be another reason for her visits.

One day she asked, "Do you think Dad knew he was gay when he married Mom?"

"No, I don't think so. He told me his only clue might have been a dream he had in college. He loved your mother."

"What about you, Adrian? When did you know?"

"I always knew. From as early as people know these things. I can't put an exact date on it, but it would have been in grade school sometime."

"What made you think . . ." Jocelyn's voice trailed off, but he understood the question.

"Oh, movies, TV shows, magazines. I always looked at the men. One day, it struck me. Other guys looked at women."

"What did you think? Did you tell anyone?"

"No, even at that age, I knew enough to keep those feelings under wraps."

Jocelyn persisted. "Did you have a feeling you were, you know, different somehow? Even before that?"

Aha, so that was it. "Is that how you feel, Jocelyn? Different?"

No answer.

"Do you think you're gay?" He searched her face for the truth.

Her flushed cheeks gave the answer, but she studied her short fingernails before looking up. "Yes. You may have zoned in on the guys, but for me it was women. I didn't think it was a big deal until I turned twelve, and all my girlfriends were crazy for guys. I knew I didn't feel like they did. Then the dreams started. Always about women. The beauty of their bodies. The smell of their hair. The feel of their soft skin. All that stuff. But I never figured Dad was gay, and now I wonder if he knew about me."

Adrian considered the possibility. "No, I'm sure your dad didn't know. He would've mentioned it to me."

Jocelyn looked at her hands again. "Dad didn't know about me, and I didn't know about him." A tear oozed from the corner of her eye. Embarrassed, she brushed it away.

Adrian had risen from his chair to sit on the sofa beside her. "Jocelyn, I think he knows, and he'd be pleased you and I are friends."

*   *   *

"Yoo-hoo, Earth to Adrian," Jocelyn sang out. "We're in Central Park, remember?"

"Sorry, Jocelyn. I was thinking." He smiled at her.

"So will you tell your mother you stretched the truth? Apologize?"

"Not a chance." Jocelyn's green eyes blazed. "What I said doesn't happen to be true, but it might be. Mom needs to get with it, move on. She's so stuck, she drives everyone nuts."

"I'm sorry," Adrian's voice was gentle. "I sincerely hope she'll find some joy in her life again. Soon."

"Yup, me, too." Jocelyn's face was glum. "Don't hold your breath, though."

"How's your golf game?"

Jocelyn groaned. "Hardly ever get to a course or driving range anymore. That's the only thing I miss about school. The chance to play lots of golf."

"If you went back in the fall, could you resume your golf scholarship?" Adrian tried to sound unconcerned.

"Yes, the team coach still calls. If I could figure out what I want to do, maybe I'd return, but nothing appeals to me. Sitting in classes bores me. I'm good, but not good enough at golf to make the pro circuit. So that means I have to figure out a career."

"You're good enough to do whatever you want if you want it bad enough. But I know what you mean. You have to have a career to fall back on if you go in for pro sports. I know a place that does extensive interest and aptitude testing. Let me know if you want the phone number. Maybe it could help."

"Maybe." Jocelyn sounded dejected for a moment then flashed a smile at Adrian. "Hey, you golf."

"Sure. Want to play when the weather improves?"

"Yes, I'd like that."

"Good, we'll do it." Adrian looked at his watch. "Time to head back? I'm cold, what about you?"

Jocelyn nodded, and they turned around.

CHAPTER 12

Margaret leaned back in the brown leather chair on her side of the large mahogany desk.

"Interesting." She ran a hand absently over her blond hair as if to smooth it though not a strand escaped from the tightly secured french twist. "What do you think, Karen?"

Karen winced in part because of her daughter's situation but also because, once again, Margaret was noncommittal. What else was new?

"I don't know whether to believe her or not," Karen said. "I think it's tied to Ari. You know, a sympathetic reaction or something. Is that possible?"

Margaret narrowed her eyes. "Sometimes," she said slowly, "a child can have a period of confusion about their sexual identity when a parent comes out as gay. But usually it's a short period of time, and the child is younger than Jocelyn." Margaret made a half smile at Karen before continuing. "However, Jocelyn indicates she's known since grade school."

"Known? How could she know at that age? I never thought about what I was when I was a kid."

"Exactly," said Margaret, shifting in her seat to adjust the skirt of her tight-fitting gray tweed suit. "Because you weren't out of line with society's expectations. You were precisely as your parents, your teachers, everyone around you expected you to be. Naturally, you didn't give it a thought. It's the person who is not what society expects who feels something is different about them."

Karen's voice was bitter. "It never occurred to Ari, or so he told me."

"Do you believe he did know and married you anyway?"

"I don't know," Karen answered miserably. "All those years . . ." Her voice broke off. Wait, she didn't want to get sidetracked. "Never mind," she continued. "What I'm asking is, do you think gayness can be inherited? Could Jocelyn have inherited it from Ari?"

Again, Margaret made a half smile. "Studies have been done on that subject. There isn't any evidence that gayness is inherited. Nor does it appear that anyone can be influenced to be gay. One person out of every ten is gay, according to some studies. And one person in ten would mean that the odds are pretty good that at least one person in every extended family could be gay."

"Oh, those studies," Karen made a brushing motion with her hand. "Just about anything can be proven with a study. As a teacher, I'm in a position to know. Every five years, someone comes out with another theory, which the higher-ups decide needs to be implemented. Studies. They come, and they go."

"Let's get back to you, Karen. Ari's been gone two years now. Have you considered dating? Now, or at some point in the future?"

"Dating!" Karen scoffed. "Who'd want to date a fat, frumpy forty-something school teacher?"

"Is that how you think of yourself?" Her leather chair squeaked as Margaret rose and walked toward the antique pendulum clock on the wall.

Karen looked down at her ample thighs then noted her therapist's trim figure from behind as Margaret wound the clock. "It's beyond pleasantly plump here. I know I need to lose weight, but I just don't get around to it. Anyway, I doubt there are many bachelors around, even if I were interested in dating. Which I'm not. Men. One was enough."

Margaret turned from the clock to face Karen. "What are you doing with your spare time these days?"

"What spare time? I'm at school till all hours. I barely have time to keep up with housework on weekends. I used to enjoy fussing with my roses, but since Ari died, I've been letting the yard service do everything."

"What do you do for fun?" Margaret had returned to her chair.

"Fun? Hmmm. I do a crossword puzzle once in a while. Watch a bit of television. Visit with my kids, I suppose, on the phone or at home. Although it hasn't been much fun lately, with Jocelyn in her obnoxious mode and Drew in a fog."

"Tell me, have you ever considered getting a pet? A puppy, perhaps?"

"A dog? Good grief, no. When would I have time to look after a dog? No, we've never had pets with both Ari and me working. Oh, Jocelyn had hamsters for a while, and Drew had goldfish when he was little."

"What about a kitten? Cats are more independent, require less care."

"There's a cat next door." She could not help but smile. "Igor is kind of a neighborhood responsibility. We all watch out for him. If I had anything, it would be a dog, but as I said, I don't have the time. It wouldn't be fair to the dog." She felt her eyes mist over. "Drew always wanted a puppy, though . . ."

Margaret glanced at the clock and stood once more. "Good session today, Karen," she said with a well-practiced smile. "I'll walk you to the elevator."

"Oh, sure," mumbled Karen. She compared her wristwatch to the clock on the wall. It was ten minutes to the hour. Not a moment too soon.

CHAPTER 13

"*Too soon*," *he says. "Let's not ruin it by making love too soon. We'll do it someday. When it's right.*"

She's grateful. She's never made love, wants it to be special, with the right person.

"*Something's wrong with him,*" *her sorority friends say.*

But she knows nothing is wrong. He's sensitive, romantic, moral. Old-fashioned. All she's dreamed of in a man.

One day, they are caught in a rainstorm, both of them soaked through. He takes her to his small room, hands her a towel to dry off and his big sweater to keep warm.

She removes her wet clothes in the bathroom, dries herself, wraps her things in a bundle. She puts on his sweater and nothing else, walks back into the room.

His eyes light up.

"*When someday comes,*" *he says softly, "I want you to wear that.*"

"*Someday is here,*" *she says, her eyes mirroring his.*

They kiss.

"*Will you give me a massage?*" *she asks, surprised at her own bravery.*

"*Yes,*" *he says. "If you're sure.*"

"*I'm sure,*" *she says.*

They kiss again, and he leads her to his bed. Not taking his eyes from her, he removes first his own clothes, then the sweater, pulling it over her head. They lie together a long time, holding each other.

"Turn over," he says at last. She lies on her stomach, he moves his warm, smooth hands over her body, first her neck, then her shoulders, then her buttocks, gently, tenderly. He kisses her neck, whispers, "I love you, Karen."

She rolls onto her back, pulls him down to kiss his lips. "And I love you, Ari Antilla."

Slowly, tenderly, he enters her. At last. She's wanted this for a long time.

CHAPTER 14

Colin and Drew, each carrying a six-pack, knocked on the door of Bob Clayton's elegant Tudor home. This massive 1920s home was near the shore, just minutes away from the New Haven Yacht Club. Colin and Bob were in the same accounting class, and Bob had invited some friends over for a party. Colin had convinced Drew to take his Mustang, probably to guarantee a sober driver for the trip home.

In a weak moment, Drew agreed. He knew he needed to be more social. He'd soon be in the business world. Hopefully. Earlier, the party had seemed like a good idea, but now it was a pain in the ass. He should have stayed home and watched TV or read or even slept.

A smiling blue-jeaned guy with a beer in hand opened the door. "Hey, Colin, good to see you." He nodded his head toward Drew. "Who's your friend?"

"This is Drew Antilla, my roommate. Drew, meet Bob Clayton." Colin spoke without enthusiasm as he strode past Bob into the house.

"Hey, Drew, make yourself at home. Put your beer in the fridge. The kitchen's the first door on the left."

Drew looked around for a place to put his jacket, finally deciding to add it to the others heaped on the bench in the large entryway. Music blared from the room at the end of the hall. He winced. Heavy metal, not his favorite. In the kitchen, Drew opened a beer and found a place for the remaining five in the fridge.

The last time he'd been to a party was more than two years ago. He looked around. Colin and Bob were on the other side of the room with a group of guys, laughing and telling stories. Here he was, a betta alone in its private bowl looking through the glass at the other fish in the big tank.

He followed the music down the hardwood hallway to the opened french doors of an ornate room with floor-to-ceiling white-paned windows. Two couples danced in their private worlds on a rose-colored Oriental carpet. A few other people sat in the floral upholstered chairs and on the matching sofa, but no one paid any attention to him. He spotted a straight-backed chair in the corner and decided to sit there.

He set his beer down and stared at the thick glass surface of the table. The betta may have been alone on his side of the glass, but he was in a worse place. Trapped in the glass between worlds, not on one side or the other.

As he watched the couples dance, Drew remembered his parents talking about how they loved to dance when they were in college.

He picked up his beer to take a long swallow. Too bad his dad hadn't left his mom alone, so she could've married someone else, someone who'd always be faithful to her, someone who wouldn't turn out to be gay.

He sighed. Then maybe he would've been someone who could handle things better. Or maybe he wouldn't even have existed.

Colin poked his nose around the french doors, "Hey, want another beer?"

"Uh, sure." Colin was certainly being hospitable. It wasn't like him.

When Colin returned with the beer, a curly-haired blonde in tight jeans and a fuzzy red top came from behind and latched onto both of their arms.

"Hey, guys, who wants to dance? And give this party some fucking life?" She flashed a mouthful of pretty white teeth. "Haven't met either of you. I'm Grace Van Gilder."

"Excuse me," said Colin, shaking her off as if she were a yappy pup. "I'm going back to the kitchen. Drew likes to dance. I need a few beers first. Go for it, Drew."

Grace clung to Drew's arm. Her smile was disarming. He had nowhere to escape.

"Let's dance!" She tugged at his arm to lead him to the dancing area. It was obvious from her syrupy expression that she'd been there a while.

"Great party," said Grace, holding his gaze. "How do you know Bob?"

"I don't," Drew responded, stuck in her warm molasses eyes. "Colin, the guy that just left, is my roommate, and they're friends. How about you? How do you know Bob?"

Grace laughed. "We're neighbors."

Drew hated to make small talk, especially over loud music. He tried to stop dancing, but Grace kept on.

She wriggled her breasts and hips. "Great beat, don't you think? Makes me want to m-o-v-e." Her warmth brushed against him as their feet scuffed the carpet.

"Hey, what's your major?" she asked.

"Economics and finance." Drew wished she would quit talking and just dance. Her imploring eyes suggested she was devoted to him, at least for the length of a music track.

"What about you?" he asked.

"I'm only a sophomore. Haven't made up my mind. A lawyer maybe. Here's a slow song." Grace pulled Drew close, pushing her breasts into his chest. To his annoyance, he felt himself get hard. Drew wondered what his dad had felt when he danced with his mom. In college, after college, before Adrian came along.

They danced, song after song, fast and slow, Grace gripping him tightly. Finally, she released him to push a wavy lock from her eyes. "I'm getting warm," she said, still clinging to his arm with the other hand. "You want to sit down?"

She reminded him of a small, golden-haired cocker spaniel. "Sounds good. But first, I could use another beer. How about you?"

"Yes, I'll join you." She trailed after him as he left the room.

The kitchen was cool. Someone had opened a window, no doubt to get rid of the smell of sweaty bodies and stale beer.

"Drew, come on over and meet some of the guys," Colin called from the butler's pantry on the other side of the room.

Relieved to hear Colin's voice, Drew answered, "Be right over." *Maybe Grace would attach herself to someone else.* He took a cold bottle from the fridge and twisted off the cap, anticipating the first spicy gulp of a fresh beer.

"Hey, what about me?" Grace demanded.

"Oh, I'm sorry," Drew replied. He hadn't meant to forget. He handed Grace a beer and walked past the extensive cherry cabinetry to Colin's area, hoping Grace would disappear.

Colin made a sweeping gesture with his arm that took in the group of five guys he was talking with. "Everyone, meet Drew, my roommate. Drew, meet everyone." He was so friendly that Drew wondered whether Colin was getting low on beer.

He listened as Colin and his friends guffawed and told stories about a professor, one Drew had never had. Grace continued to look up at him. He tried to ignore her and listen to the stories, but everyone was talking at once, and he didn't find the anecdotes as funny as they did.

Bob came up behind him and slapped him on the shoulder. "How goes it, Drew?"

"Great. Glad I came," Drew lied.

"If you're tired of these guys, we've got pool going in the game room downstairs." Bob certainly tried to be a great host.

"Thanks, but I'm not much of a pool player," Drew apologized. He felt like a social dud. "I'll just hang out in the living room in front of the TV, if that's okay." He pointed to a room across the hall from the kitchen.

"Actually, that's the study," Grace interjected. "Living room's on the other side of the house."

"Okay," said Drew, "the study then."

Grace followed him across the hall to a warm-looking room with book-lined shelves, a marble fireplace, leather furniture, and a small TV in the corner. Drew chose a place on the couch, and she nestled in next to him. An old movie was playing. The music from the other room was low. The party was quieting down. Some people had already left.

"Hey, Drew, you want to take a walk upstairs?" slurred Grace. Her hand rubbed his thigh. "There's five bedrooms up there. I bet we could find a place to, you know, be alone." She took his hand and placed it between her legs.

Drew was throbbing now. "No, I don't think so. I'm not prepared. Don't have anything with me." He tried to sound nonchalant, worldly. But god, what did she think? He hardly knew her. He gently pulled his hand away.

"I thought you liked me, Drew."

"Well, I do. But still . . ." Why couldn't he tell the truth? He didn't want to, even if his body argued. When he made love, he wanted to be with someone special, not someone he just met.

Drew concentrated on the TV. Grace fell asleep, nuzzling into him, her head resting on his shoulder. She was still there an hour later when Colin finally appeared.

"Ready to go, Drew? I've had too many beers."

"Sure." Extricating his arm, he found a few pillows to use as a headrest for Grace, figuring she'd find her way home eventually since she lived down the street.

"I'm ready to go too. Had a great time." He knew Colin wouldn't remember the lie tomorrow.

CHAPTER 15

A soft rain began to fall as Jocelyn approached D'Agostino's Supermarket. D'Agostino markets were a longtime New York City tradition dating back to the 1930s. Their stores offered a wide variety of groceries along with baked goods and a deli, all under the same roof. Jocelyn needed a few items but had to be at work in an hour. Not bothering with a handbasket, she dashed up and down the narrow aisles, grabbing as she went—tuna, bread, two cans of soup, crackers. *What else? Milk and cheese.* She rounded the corner on the way to the dairy section. *Bam*—she collided with someone in a bright red jacket coming the other way. Jocelyn's armload clattered to the floor.

"I'm sorry," she said to the woman. "I'm in too much of a hurry. Are you okay?"

"I'm fine," the young blonde replied with a lopsided grin. "Here, let me help you."

They both crouched at the same time, bumping each other again. They laughed, holding their heads.

Startled green eyes gazed into wise blue, and the groceries remained on the floor while the women rose to their feet as if in a trance. Jocelyn felt her skin heat up. The woman's wink was as brief as the twitch of a whisker, but Jocelyn caught it.

"Hi. I'm Jocelyn Antilla. You live around here?" Jocelyn couldn't believe she'd just said that.

"No, but I work at Lenox Hill Hospital," came the reply. "My name's Lisa. Lisa Michaelson."

Remembering her limited time, Jocelyn glanced at her watch.

"Oh, no. I have to get to work." She knelt again to pick up her groceries, forgetting the milk and cheese. Lisa followed her to the checkout counter, picking up a bag of corn chips on the way. Jocelyn studied their reflection in the mirror over the cash register. They were about the same height, both with medium blunt-cut hairstyles. Lisa's sleek hair was swept back while Jocelyn's own tumbled forward.

"Do you like movies?" asked Lisa, lightly brushing against her arm.

"Sure," said Jocelyn. Her throat tightened as she tried to contain the bubble of anticipation rising in her chest.

"Want to see one tonight?"

"Can't. Have to work."

Lisa's face deflated.

"What about Sunday night?" Jocelyn offered. "I'm off then."

"Great," Lisa said, her smile resurfacing. "Seven o'clock at the Apollo?"

"Sure. Sounds good." Jocelyn's hands trembled as she reached for her sack. She hoped Lisa didn't notice. "Maybe we can go for coffee or a drink later."

The crooked grin emerged again. "All right. See you soon. Nice bumping into you." That wink again.

Jocelyn soared home, her feet barely grazing the wet sidewalk. As she put her groceries away, she relived every giddy detail of the encounter.

Wait. She'd just agreed to meet a mysterious woman for an unnamed movie. Who knew what was playing? Or even if there was a movie at seven. *Come to think of it, what was her name? Oh yeah, Lisa Michaels. No, not Michaels. Michaelson.*

Jocelyn left for work in a fog wondering how she could wait the two days until Sunday.

CHAPTER 16

Drew stared at the backs of warehouses flashing by as the train sped toward Manhattan on Saturday morning. Last Tuesday, he'd phoned Jocelyn on the spur of the moment and invited himself to her apartment for the weekend. They wouldn't have much time together, considering Jocelyn had to work tonight, but at least it would be more than they'd had in Stamford. He missed Josey.

For the first hour, thoughts rolled through his head in glimpses, like the buildings going by. His father. When did he change? The man he knew, gone, even before the funeral.

The funeral. The viewing. He and Jocelyn propped up between their mother and Granbo. His mother like a robot, saying the same words. Over and over.

"Yes, a tragedy. So young. A shock to everyone. We'll manage."

His grandmother, consoling everyone. Even through her tears. Everyone except his mother.

Manage. She'd said they'd manage. Two years later he was managing, but his mother wasn't. And Jocelyn? He didn't know.

Exhausted by the effort to sort it out, he leaned back and closed his eyes for the last half hour of the ride, wishing he could lose himself in the rhythmic clinkety-clank of metal against metal.

"Penn Station," the conductor droned through the speaker box as the train slowed. "Last stop."

Drew snatched up his backpack and flowed with the current of people leaving the train. He rode the escalator to street level and waited his turn for a cab to ferry him across town to Jocelyn's apartment. When he arrived, the doorman buzzed to let her know he was on his way.

Before he could knock, Jocelyn opened the door of the third floor apartment. "Glad to see you, Drew." She hugged him. "You're early. I didn't expect you until later. Hey, nice haircut. You've been to Granbo's."

"Sure have," said Drew as he strolled in.

Jocelyn ran a hand through her hair. "I've got to see her soon too. My hair's getting long."

Drew inspected the living room. "I haven't been here since Dad died, but it looks pretty much the same." He'd always loved the hardwood floor that peeked out from the sides of the Oriental carpet, the crystal chandelier, and the fireplace.

Jocelyn shrugged. "No major changes. I put up a few posters in the bedroom. That's about it. I still think of it as Mom and Dad's place in the city, not mine. Mom never stops letting me know how grateful I should be to live here."

Hearing the blare of a car horn outside, Drew looked out the window for a moment before turning back to his sister. "Let's not talk about Mom for a while."

"Fine, but she pisses me off. I'm ready to tell her she can have this fucking apartment, and I'll find my own place."

Drew could feel his shoulders tense.

Jocelyn sighed, "Okay. I'll stop."

"Thanks." With a wry smile, Drew plopped into the brocade sofa, tossing his backpack on the floor. "Definitely more comfortable than the ancient sofa in my place."

Jocelyn grinned. "Maybe it's worth enduring Mom's rants."

Drew gave her a warning look. They laughed, and Jocelyn settled onto the couch beside him.

After they'd chatted for a short time, Jocelyn jumped up and began to pace. "Let's not waste our day sitting around. How about a walk?"

Drew smirked. "I see you haven't changed. Always on the go. Me, I could spend lots of time lying around."

"Let's take a cab to Times Square and work our way back through Rockefeller Center."

"Sounds like a plan," said Drew, standing up, ready to go. He hadn't taken off his ski jacket.

Jocelyn retrieved her parka and fanny pack from the hall closet. "We'll find a deli to have a bite to eat later. We have the afternoon to hang out before I have to get ready for work at six. Sorry I have to work, by the way. I tried to get tonight off."

Drew pulled his gloves out of his pocket. "That's okay, I'll find something to do."

They left the cozy apartment and prepared to face the brisk March air as they hailed a cab.

"I haven't seen Times Square in a while," said Drew. "I think the last time was that weekend we all came to see *Phantom of the Opera*."

"Yeah, I remember," Jocelyn said. "Nice memory."

CHAPTER 17

S he feels his chest against her back as his soothing voice drifts over her.
"It'll be all right, pussycat," he says.

"Ari!" Karen's eyes flew open. "Blast him." Why couldn't she get that man out of her life? The too familiar sobs claimed her body once more. She cried until she was sure the soggy pillow couldn't hold another tear then turned it over, as if to get a fresh start.

She raised her head to look at the clock. Two hours and forty minutes until she would meet Siri for lunch. Time enough to pull herself together, thank God. She threw the covers back and got out of bed.

*   *   *

Karen surveyed the graceful surroundings of the Italian restaurant. The interior was elegant but warm, with crisp white linen tablecloths, delicate crystal glasses, and framed watercolor paintings of Tuscany on the wall. They'd started with wine but weren't in a hurry to order lunch. "We haven't met like this for years."

"You're right," agreed Siri.

Karen swirled the dark ruby-colored cabernet in her goblet then inhaled the aroma of currants and blackberries. Instantly, she was a child again, sampling sweet berries with her mother in the garden on a hot summer day. When she took a sip, the acrid taste surprised her.

"Is there a particular reason you wanted to meet?" she asked.

"You're so direct, Karen," said Siri, scrutinizing her with luminous green eyes from across the table. "Yes, there is a reason I suggested lunch. There's something I want to talk to you about. I'm not sure how I should begin."

"Just plunge in," Karen advised. "Not much could shock me these days."

A shadow of uncertainty crossed Siri's face, but she continued. "I'm sure that's true," she said. "Karen, you've mentioned your therapist. Margaret, is it?"

"Yes, that's her name." Karen's eyes narrowed. "What about Margaret?"

"You never have much good to say about her. And it's been over two years . . ." Siri's voice trailed off.

Karen set her wine glass down. "What are you getting at? That Margaret is useless, or that I'm a psychological mess?"

"Oh, Karen. That's not it. But I confess, I've wondered at the wisdom of you continuing with a therapist who doesn't listen. Honestly, I think you should consider something else."

Siri stopped speaking, but Karen sensed she had more to say. "Yes? What is it?"

It was Siri's turn to take a swallow of wine, the sleeve of her taupe chenille jacket brushing the tablecloth as she leaned forward. "I was wondering if you'd ever considered a group."

"Group therapy?" Karen tried not to grimace. "Forget it. I went that route once. For an entire month, I listened to people moan and blather on. I just couldn't relate."

"That sounds like a group organized for grief. That's not the kind I meant."

"No? Well, what then? I'm confused." Karen stared at her.

Siri squirmed in her chair like a shy child in the principal's office. "I know how private you are about things, and this is something you've never mentioned. But, Karen, I know. Ari was gay."

Karen felt the blood rush to her face. "But I haven't said—"

Siri interrupted. Her voice was gentle. "I know you haven't. But people talk."

Karen looked at the napkin in her lap. "Who knows? The entire staff?"

"Probably. It's been mentioned by a few people. Not as much now as it used to be."

Karen raised her head. "Mr. McKinley? Does John know?"

Siri shrugged. "Probably, but I've never heard him say anything. I've never been involved in any conversation, actually. I've just listened. I'm only bringing this up because I think you might need some additional help, and I have a suggestion."

Karen felt lightheaded, like she was dropping in an elevator. "How long have people known?"

Siri's lucid eyes continued to hold her gaze. "Since shortly after the funeral."

"Oh, god." Karen covered her face with her napkin. "I can imagine them all, gossiping, pitying. Blaming me, probably."

"No," Siri said emphatically. "People were not mean-spirited. Oh, it was a shock, and people felt bad for you, but they understood. Let me get back to my point. I'm bringing this up not to let you know who knows what but to suggest a possible course of action for you."

"Oh?" Karen's queasiness persisted.

"Yes. You've heard me speak of Bridget, my neighbor."

"The one with the five kids?"

"Right. Well, Bridget has a married brother." Siri settled back into her chair and continued. "All seemed well in his marriage until he came across some letters that proved, in no uncertain terms, that his wife was having an affair with a woman friend. The discovery devastated him. His wife moved out to be with her lover, and the kids shuffled back and forth between homes. The poor man was a mess until someone introduced him to a group for the straight spouses of homosexuals. At the first meeting, he found out he was not the only person this had ever happened to, there was a whole roomful of people. The group saved him, according to Bridget." Siri paused to take another sip of wine.

"Interesting." Karen was paying attention, but she still felt faint.

Siri set her glass down and opened her suede handbag to remove a piece of paper. She handed it to Karen. "Here's the name of a person you can call about a similar group. It's not Bridget's brother's group. He lives in the Midwest. But it's a group in this area recommended by his facilitator. I asked Bridget to get this information for me. I told her it was for a friend, but I didn't say who."

Karen folded the piece of paper carefully and placed it inside her own purse. "Thank you," she managed to choke out. "I'll think about what you said." The sound of her voice seemed far off. She felt as if she were floating.

CHAPTER 18

S *he floats down the aisle on her father's arm in her flowing white satin gown. Showers of red roses, baby's breath, and gardenias cascade from her hands.*

Left foot glides, close, pause. Right foot glides, close, pause.

She savors the exotic sweet scent of the gardenias, the most fragrant of all flowers.

Left foot glides, close, pause. Right foot glides, close, pause.

The vibrant trumpet tones of the processional echo through the church as she walks past her family and smiling-faced guests.

Left foot glides, close, pause. Right foot glides, close, pause.

Ari waits at the front, a boutonniere of two roses and baby's breath in the lapel of his white tuxedo. He wears no gardenias.

Left foot glides, close, pause. Right foot glides, close, pause.

She sees the tears in her father's eyes as he presents her to the groom. Ari's eyes shimmer when he holds out his arm to lead her to the chrysanthemum-laden altar. They face the minister, and the ceremony begins.

"I, Ari, take you, Karen, to be my wedded wife, to have and to hold from this day forward, for richer or poorer, in sickness and in health, to love and to cherish, until death do us part."

His voice is tender but strong. Her answer is subdued but clear.

"I, Karen, take you, Ari, to be my wedded husband, to have and to hold from this day forward, for richer or poorer, in sickness and in health, to love and to cherish, until death do us part."

The minister says, "I pronounce you husband and wife."

Their eyes unite, their lips melt. The kiss is velvet.

"Ladies and gentlemen, I present to you Mr. and Mrs. Ari Antilla."

As she turns, an intoxicating gardenia scent envelops her. She knows the roses and baby's breath will endure, but the gardenias will wilt before the day is done.

CHAPTER 19

Jocelyn and Drew walked to Times Square, people watching and exploring as they went. They poked around in small shops, visited the NBC store, and walked past the neon lights of the news boards and Broadway theaters.

"I feel anonymous here, but in a good way," Drew said as they navigated the swarming sidewalks.

"I know. It's freeing somehow," said Jocelyn as she studied her brother. "I love this city. It pulses with life and action, never rests, never sleeps. It's alive. Every neighborhood has its own charm and rhythm."

"I like it too," said Drew, "but as much as I'm enjoying it right now, I'm not sure I could live here. The lights, the billboards, the fancy restaurants, and hotels are overwhelming after a while. Not to mention the crowds, the horns honking, the sirens blaring. Does anyone ever slow down?"

Jocelyn tossed an impish grin his way. "Sure. You can always veg out on a bench in Central Park and watch the rest of the city pass by on foot. Or bikes or skates."

"True enough. I guess there's a place for everyone."

"I'm starved. Let's get a bite to eat," Jocelyn said, looking around. "McHale's is in the next block. Their hamburgers are great. It's one of the best kept secrets in town. Lots of stagehands and theater people hang out there."

"Good idea," Drew answered. "I'm hungry too."

They entered the bar, and the hostess seated them at a corner table in the open area at the back. After studying the menu, Jocelyn ordered a mushroom burger and small salad while Drew ordered a double cheeseburger with fries.

"We have to get together more often, Drew, one way or another. I've missed you."

"Me too," said Drew as he gobbled his sandwich. "The food here is awesome."

"Should we have dessert? Their cheesecake is even better than Mom's."

"You're kidding. Can't believe that. You have the cheesecake. I'll have a piece of that Black Forest torte I saw when we came in."

Jocelyn reached across the table to ruffle his hair. "Sure you will," she said. "You never miss a chance, do you? You've always been the chocolate lover in the family."

A solemn shadow fell over Drew's face. "Josey, I miss what we had as a family. You know, the way it was before. A time of innocence."

Jocelyn couldn't miss the hurt in his voice. "I know." She wished to her very core that she could somehow take her brother's pain away.

"Hey, let's do something fun this afternoon," she said. "Like skating at Rockefeller Center. You want to?"

"Sure."

To her relief, a glimmer of a smile appeared on his face. After their dessert, they set off for the arena to rent skates.

"I haven't skated in at least five years," Drew said as he finished tying his laces.

Jocelyn stood, ready to go. "Me neither. This'll be fun."

"It was such a family thing," Drew said, following her onto the ice. "Mom and Dad, all of us skating together."

Jocelyn coasted beside her brother, listening to the scraping sounds on the ice as they circled the arena. Finally, she thought of something to change the subject. "Remember how you taught me to skate? You skated backwards in front of me and pulled me along."

"It didn't take long for you to become a better skater than me."

"That's not true." Jocelyn couldn't believe how down on himself Drew was these days. Trying to sound cheerful she said, "Hey, let's do it. Skate backwards in front of me, okay?"

Drew hesitated. "Don't know if I still can. I'll try, I guess."

He took Jocelyn's hands, turned around, and pulled her along. He seemed very unsure.

"I'll watch out for people," Jocelyn said. "Keep going. Don't turn around."

"I don't like it when I can't see where I'm going."

"Trust me. I'll watch the ice."

After one tour around, Jocelyn let go of his hands. "Enough of this. Let's do something different. Let's pretend we're dancers." She glided away. "Like . . . like this." She put her hands above her head and twirled around on one skate. "I bet you can't do that."

Drew glanced around at the other skaters. "You want me to look like some kind of wimp?"

"For god's sake, Drew. You don't know a soul here."

Drew hesitated a moment, then screwed his lips in determination. He pushed off on his skates, quickly gathering momentum. He twirled around not once but three times. Jocelyn was flabbergasted.

"Show off! Let me try that." She skated off ahead of him and made one pirouette before falling onto the ice. Flat.

Drew rushed to her side. "Josey, are you okay?"

Only her pride was injured. "Yes, I'm fine," she said laughing. "Help me up."

Drew pulled her to her feet and helped her brush off her jeans and jacket. They skated off again, hand in hand, both facing forward. They laughed and giggled like fourth-grade kids for the next half hour until Jocelyn recalled she had to go to work.

"Omigosh, look at the time," she said, consulting her watch. "I've got to get back."

"One more time around before we leave?"

She looked at her older brother in surprise. Was he pleading? She reached out to stroke his cheek with her hand. "Sure," she said gently. "Could be ages before we have another chance."

*   *   *

Back in the apartment, Jocelyn wished she didn't have to go to work. She worried about Drew. "What will you do while I'm gone?" she asked, trying to sound nonchalant.

Drew peered up from his relaxed position on the couch. "I brought along my book and notes to study for my exam." He paged through his notebook. "I'll be fine. Where's the remote for the TV?"

Jocelyn picked up the remote from the end table. She handed it to Drew then gathered her jacket from the back of a chair. "If there's anything you want from the refrigerator, help yourself."

Drew clicked on the TV and began to flip through the channels. "I doubt I'll be hungry after our big lunch, but thanks for the offer."

Jocelyn remembered that Drew had always escaped into TV. She doubted he'd study. "Okay, I'm on my way. I'll be back about midnight."

*   *   *

When Jocelyn returned from work six hours later, the smell of stale beer greeted her at the door. The television blared.

"Drew, I'm home." No answer. Walking into the living room, she found him lying on the couch, surrounded by empty beer cans. "Are you awake?" Still no answer. Alarmed, she shook his shoulders and spoke louder. "Wake up!"

His eyes glassy, he slurred, "What's up? I must have fallen asleep. What time . . . ?"

She sat next to him. "Hell, Drew. You scared me for a minute. Fallen asleep? I guess so! Did you have a party or something?" She glanced at the cans on the floor.

Drew spoke haltingly. "No party. Just me and my book. I studied a while, saw the beer. Didn't think you'd mind. Watched TV."

"You're drunk."

He pulled himself to a halfhearted slouch. "Not drunk, Josey. Promise. I'll be okay. I should have cleaned up."

He got to his feet and zigzagged across the living room to the bathroom. Jocelyn watched him, wishing again she'd been able to stay home. Moments later, he returned and plunked back down next to her on the couch.

She put a hand on his shoulder. "This isn't like you. I never thought I'd come home and find this."

Drew pushed her hand away. "Knock it off, Josey. I was thinking. Mom and Dad shouldn't have had children. Everything turned out so wrong."

"No, Drew, it didn't." Jocelyn put her hand on his shoulder again. He didn't resist this time. "I'm worried about you. You shouldn't think like that."

"I'm okay. Just tired now. Want to sleep." He stood up and staggered to the bathroom again.

Jocelyn counted nine beer cans as she gathered them to throw in the kitchen trash. While Drew was in the bathroom, she quickly prepared the sofa bed with sheets, a wool blanket, and a fluffy down pillow. Her brother's behavior disturbed her, but she was determined not to sound like her mother. "All right, bro. The bed's ready. Sleep well. I'm tired myself. See you in the morning."

She walked to her bedroom without looking back.

CHAPTER 20

Drew awoke to the clatter of pots and pans and the smell of something cooking in the kitchen. God, what a splitting headache he had. He slipped on his clothes from the day before and groped his way to the bathroom, stepping carefully to avoid jarring his head. The mirror reflected puffy red eyes and a two-day beard growth. He'd forgotten to shave yesterday. He slapped water on his face to freshen it, but it didn't help. Maybe Jocelyn's mint-flavored mouthwash would get the fuzzy taste out of his mouth.

In the kitchen, he discovered Jocelyn making french toast. His stomach heaved at the thought. "Don't fuss, Jocelyn. I'm not very hungry." Queasy, he pulled out a chair to sit at the kitchen table.

"Oh, no trouble. Usually I just have cereal. But because you're here I decided to do something different. You woke up just in time." Jocelyn placed a plate in front of him with two pieces of french toast slathered with butter and maple syrup then dished up one for herself and sat in the chair opposite. She'd already put two glasses of orange juice on the table.

"How are you doing this morning?" she asked, eating energetically.

"I'm okay." He forced himself to take a bite of the french toast.

"How's everything at school? Classes okay?"

"Yeah. Things are fine."

"Dating anyone?"

Damn, now Jocelyn was sounding like Mom. Why did they both worry about his social life? "I'm getting out. I went to a party the other night. One of Colin's friends."

"Great."

Drew added, "I met a girl there. Her name is Grace. She's been calling me since the party."

Jocelyn smiled. "Just phone calls? You haven't asked her out?"

Drew shifted in his chair and considered whether or not to try a sip of orange juice. "No. Not yet." Grace had telephoned him three times during the past week. Each time he'd made an excuse why they couldn't get together.

Jocelyn shrugged. "Well, let me know if you do. I'm always interested. I met a girl too. Lisa. Getting together with her tonight for a movie."

Drew felt uncomfortable talking to Jocelyn about her date with a woman, so he said nothing. It was her life, but right now he'd rather not talk about it. At least she figured it out early, not like Dad.

He pushed his plate away. "I think I better get back to Hartford. I still have to study."

"Darn. I'm free for the rest of the day. I thought you were staying."

"Sorry. I think I should catch the eleven o'clock."

Jocelyn looked disappointed. "Okay, if you say so. Maybe you can study on the train. It was fun having you around this weekend. Felt like old times."

"I'll come visit again. Soon. Promise."

He felt Jocelyn's eyes on him as he tossed his books and yesterday's socks into his backpack.

"I'll catch a cab back to the station," he said, giving her a quick squeeze on his way out the door.

*   *   *

Drew plopped his backpack on the seat beside him on the train. He'd had a nice time with Josey this weekend. Amazing, he could still skate backwards. As his mouth formed a grin, his head began to throb again. *Ouch.* He should have stopped sooner. Not the first time he'd drunk too much alone.

Maybe his mom and his sister were right. He should get out once in a while. Well, Grace would call again. Next time he'd be friendly. Talk longer. Invite her to a movie. It couldn't hurt. The party had been okay, and Grace, even though she talked too much, was pretty nice.

*   *   *

He tried the door to his apartment. Locked. Funny, Colin's car was here. Usually when they were home, they didn't bother to lock the door. He figured Colin would be studying or working on the major paper he had due next week. After a brief search, he found his key in the bottom of his backpack.

Drew opened the door and walked into the silent apartment. "Hey, Colin, I'm home."

No answer. Colin must be out. Someone must have picked him up, or maybe he walked to the library. But still, it was strange that his computer was on, and it looked like he was in the middle of a project with papers in various piles on the desk.

Drew emptied his backpack in his room then returned to the living room couch with his econ book. Suddenly, he heard a thump coming from the direction of the other bedroom.

"Colin, is that you?" he called. No answer. Maybe it was just a cat outside knocking something over. Or the wind. Drew continued reading his chapter.

Another thump. And then a creak. How odd. He'd better check it out. He turned the doorknob to Colin's room slowly. Something told him not to turn on the light.

Colin. He was home. In bed with someone. Two bodies together. Naked and moving. Clothing on the floor.

Colin lifted his head and peered at the open door in the dim light. "What the hell?"

Drew froze. He had to say something. He couldn't just shut the door and leave. He tried to sound matter of fact. "I didn't know you were home."

Colin clutched at the sheet. "Damn. Give us some privacy, will you?"

"Hey, didn't mean to disturb you, dude. I didn't hear you when I came in."

"For god's sake, just leave us alone."

As Drew backed out of the room and closed the door, he caught a glimpse of the other face in the bed. Her hair messed up. Grace. Colin was fucking Grace.

He clutched his stomach with both hands and ran to the toilet, but he couldn't throw up. Back in the living room, he impulsively wadded up the papers around the computer and threw them across the room. The room spun. It must be all that beer he drank last night. He had to lie down.

On unsteady feet, he hobbled to his bedroom and buried himself in his bed, covering his eyes and ears with pillows. His head throbbed. He didn't want to hear. He didn't want to see.

Drew remembered the sleeping pills the doctor had prescribed when his dad died. He'd kept them but never used them. Gripping the walls, he wove his way to the bathroom. He'd take one. Just one.

CHAPTER 21

Jocelyn waited outside the movie theatre. She must have been a fool to think Lisa had actually meant her spur-of-the-moment invitation. What in hell had she been thinking when she agreed to make herself so vulnerable? She checked the time again. 7:10. Five minutes had passed. Five more and she'd leave. A cigarette would be nice about now. Too bad she didn't smoke.

At that moment, Lisa strolled around the corner. "Bet you thought I wasn't coming," she said, with the beginnings of a sly grin. She wore snug-fitting black slacks with a leather motorcycle jacket; its toughness softened by an oversized knit collar.

"I was starting to wonder," said Jocelyn. She admired Lisa's sleek look.

"Sorry." The crooked grin spread across her face. "I'm usually on time. Have you figured out what movie we should see?"

Jocelyn was taken aback. She'd thought Lisa would have a plan. "No, I didn't think about it." She waved an arm at the sign above the ticket booth. "I guess these are our choices. Anything you want to see?"

Lisa looked over the list. "Not particularly. Maybe we could just walk around and talk? Or get some coffee somewhere?"

"Sure, where'll we go?" Suddenly, the movie wasn't important. Jocelyn sensed they both would rather talk.

"Oh, how about this way, toward the grocery store where we bumped into each other?"

Jocelyn laughed. "Fine with me." She would have cheerfully walked through an alley if that's what Lisa suggested.

The pair started walking at a brisk pace.

Lisa was the first to speak. "So Jocelyn, what do you do for a living?"

"Sheesh. You get right to the point," blurted Jocelyn. She instantly regretted the words. Hoping Lisa hadn't taken offense, she decided to be open about her situation. "I don't have a career; I'm a college dropout. I work as a waitress at Carolina's. What about you?"

"Oh, I've been to Carolina's. Good food. I'm a physical therapist," she said, with no hint of arrogance in her voice.

"That's a great job," said Jocelyn. "A lot of school, though. Do you work with elderly patients? Sports injuries?"

"Mostly sports injuries."

"Thought so," said Jocelyn, turning sideways to scrutinize Lisa better. "You look athletic."

"And so do you," returned Lisa, conducting her own inspection. "I swim, run, and bike. And you?"

"I like all sports, but golf is my passion. I was on the golf team at Wagner College before I dropped out."

"I love to watch golf on TV. I've played a bit. Took some lessons in college. I'd like to play more, but golf takes a lot of time."

"True," Jocelyn answered. They walked in silence for several steps.

"So besides golf, what do you do for fun?" Lisa asked.

"Fun? Hmmm. Fight with my mom, I guess."

Lisa laughed. "Join the club. Must be a rite of passage."

Jocelyn shivered. "Hey, I'm getting cold. When the wind blows this time of year, it feels like Siberia."

"Let's find a place to get some coffee."

Jocelyn looked around to orient herself. "We're only two blocks from my place. I fix a mean cup of hot chocolate. Can I entice you with that?"

Lisa raised an eyebrow and gazed directly into Jocelyn's eyes. "Yes, I'd like some hot chocolate. No need to try to entice me, though. You already have."

A tingling sensation spread through Jocelyn's body. She opened her mouth to speak, but nothing came out.

"I'm sorry, I shouldn't have said that," Lisa said. "Just can't resist making a crack sometimes."

"That's okay." Jocelyn nudged her head to the left. "It's this way, across the street."

Entering the apartment, Lisa peered into the living room. "Wow. Velvet drapes and such an ornate fireplace. I love the burgundy walls and all that mahogany. Fancy for a waitress."

"Yes, you're right," said Jocelyn. "Here, let me hang up your jacket. This place belongs to my family. My grandparents on my mom's side bought it for my parents when they got married, but my parents moved to Stamford when I was born. They kept the apartment though because my dad worked on Wall Street and sometimes stayed over."

"Are these your parents?" Lisa picked up a small framed photo from the table in the hallway as Jocelyn shut the closet door.

"Yes."

"Wow, your dad looks like a red-headed Mel Gibson."

"Oh? Never thought about that, but maybe he does. Or he did. Dad died two years ago in January. Cancer of the pancreas."

Lisa placed the picture back on the table carefully. "I'm sorry."

"Yeah, me too." Jocelyn allowed herself a small moment of sadness then moved on. "He was a great dad."

Lisa's voice was gentle. "It must be hard."

"Yes, it is at times. I'm okay though. I worry more about my mom and my older brother. Everyone knows Mom's having trouble because it's all she talks about. But my brother, he's just the opposite. Keeps everything inside. He was here this weekend. Left this morning."

"Are you and your brother the only kids?"

"Yup. Come in, and I'll show you a picture of Drew."

Lisa followed Jocelyn into the living room and studied the picture Jocelyn took from the mantle.

"He looks kind, yet serious," she said. "And sensitive."

"You're very perceptive."

Lisa set the first picture down and picked up another. "And who's this flashy-looking woman?"

Jocelyn broke into a grin. "That's Granbo. My dad's mother. She's a riot."

"Granbo? That's a term I haven't heard before. Makes me think of Rambo." laughed Lisa.

"Well, she is rather Rambo-like, but that's not how she got the name. When Drew was little, *Grandma* came out *Granbo*. Mom and Dad thought it was cute, so it stuck."

"Granbo," said Lisa softly. "I like it. She looks like she suits the name." She returned the picture to its place. "Hey, didn't you promise me something warm and sweet?"

Finding herself at a loss for words, Jocelyn knew she'd met her match.

CHAPTER 22

Drew emerged from his bedroom sometime after ten o'clock, thirsty and still groggy from the sleeping pill. Colin was watching television. Alone.

"Colin, what the hell were you doing with Grace?"

"Wasn't it obvious?" Colin answered, not taking his eyes from the TV. "Why the fuck did you wreck my paper? I had to reprint the whole damn thing."

"Shit, you're lucky I didn't trash the computer. Next time, I will. I asked you a question, asshole. Why was she here?"

"Grace? She phoned for you late last night. I told her you weren't home."

"So that explains it?"

Colin shrugged. "We talked a while. I told her she should come over, and we could talk some more."

"Give me a break. That wasn't talking going on in your bedroom."

"You didn't want to go out with her. When she called here last week, you fucking hardly gave her the time of day. Hell, one time when I answered the phone you told me to tell her you weren't home."

"That was my business. What does that have to do with you?"

"I got the idea you weren't interested, so what the hell. She came over last night. We talked, drank a few beers." He smirked. "Well, more than a few beers."

Drew slammed his fist into the table. "You fucked my girl."

Colin shouted, "Your girl? Like shit."

"How did you know I wouldn't change my mind?"

"Knock it off. I didn't know you cared about her. You fooled me, all right? And you came home too fucking early."

"You going to see her again?"

Colin continued to watch television. "Nope, not my type. She talks too much. And she's like a rag doll in bed."

"You're such a prick." Drew snatched the remote from the couch then turned the TV off. He removed the batteries and waved them in Colin's face. "Go fuck yourself. Manually." Drew threw the remote across the room and stormed out of the apartment, slamming the door behind him.

*   *   *

As if he hadn't walked enough this weekend, with Jocelyn in New York. As if his feet weren't sore from skating. He walked just to walk. He walked just to think. Now Grace wouldn't call him. Colin had ruined that.

He wanted to talk to someone. His mother? No, she'd talk about her same old shit. Maybe he'd call Jocelyn. No, she'd be out with her girlfriend. Maybe he'd just go home and drink the rest of Colin's beer. That bastard.

CHAPTER 23

Karen checked her faculty mailbox at the end of the day and was relieved. There weren't any pressing notes from Mr. McKinley, only a reminder about the faculty meeting tomorrow morning. She had to be at school early anyway. But right now, she wished she didn't have so many tests to correct before heading home.

It was a long walk from the office to her second floor classroom, especially in the new Naturalizer dress shoes that matched her suede dress so perfectly. As she walked, she noticed that the metal student lockers lining the hallway could use a fresh coat of paint. The tiled floors, so shiny in the morning, now were scuffed and waiting for the custodial mops to work their nightly magic.

Since Siri's classroom door was open, she decided to stop in and talk for a while before grading her papers. Siri was organizing the books and papers heaped on her desk.

"Hi, Siri, you're really attacking that desk of yours in earnest."

"Oh, hi, Karen. I can stand quite a bit of clutter, but I reached the point today where I felt this mess was about to eat me alive. I wish I knew the secret of keeping a classroom as neat and organized as yours. Maybe in another life."

Both women laughed. Siri sat at her desk, and Karen slipped into a nearby student desk.

Karen said, "You know me, Siri. My motto has always been "Everything has its place." But I know lots of people don't feel that way. By the way, in case you don't get to your mailbox tonight, don't forget about the faculty meeting tomorrow morning, seven thirty."

"Thanks, I remember writing it on my calendar, but I'd forgotten about it. What do you think the hot issues will be this time?"

Karen shrugged. "Who knows? I guess we'll find out."

"How was your day today?" Siri asked.

"I had a decent day, gave tests in a few classes, so I had more time than usual off my feet. Thank goodness. I never would have been able to stand all day in these shoes." She slipped them off gingerly.

"I learned the importance of wearing comfortable shoes the hard way," said Siri. "These leather lace-ups may not be fashionable, but they feel good on my feet."

"Speaking of comfort, that reminds me it must have been hard to bring up what you did at lunch last Saturday. I'm embarrassed that people at school know what they do, but I'm glad *you* know. It's a relief that I don't have to hide this from you."

"No problem. I'm glad you didn't mind me bringing it up."

"Not at all," Karen lowered her voice, not wanting anyone walking by to hear. "In fact, I called the number you gave me and spoke to the facilitator of the Straight Spouses of Gays group. I'm going to a session Thursday night."

Siri beamed. "Well, good for you."

"I'm a little nervous, but I'll let you know how it goes," Karen offered.

"I'm glad you feel comfortable confiding in me. I hope it's helpful."

"I appreciate that. I'll leave you to your work now and get to my algebra tests so I can leave at a decent hour."

*   *   *

Karen glanced at the clock on her classroom wall. It was five fifteen, time to go home. She'd corrected the advanced algebra tests and updated her lesson plans. She placed a stack of uncorrected assignments in her briefcase to finish at home.

As she took her coat from the closet, Roger Delacroix ambled into the room. He wore his school letter jacket and had a backpack slung over his shoulder. It was late for a student visit.

"Mrs. Antilla, can I talk to you a minute? Did you, by any chance, correct my algebra test?"

Karen put her coat back on the hook, noticing that Roger had dropped his usual cocky attitude. "As a matter of fact, I've just finished. They're on my desk." Roger followed as she walked to the front.

"Basketball practice ended, so I decided to see if you were still here," he explained.

"Oh, that's why you're at school so late. I thought there had to be a good reason. We'll take a look at your test."

Karen sifted through a stack of papers. Roger stood with his hands in his pockets looking uncharacteristically nervous.

Karen took his paper from the middle of the stack, studied it a moment, and then said, "Your grades have shown improvement in the last few weeks, Roger. Pull up a chair."

Roger dragged a chair next to her desk and flopped into it. "I have to do well in math if I want to get into engineering school so I can work for my dad. Is that my test?"

"Yes," she said, putting the test on the corner of her desk so they both could look at it.

"Eighty-three percent." Roger shook his head. "My dad will freak when he sees this." He slumped back into the chair.

"Eighty-three percent is a definite improvement over the grades you were getting at the beginning of the semester." Karen opened her grade book and showed Roger his recorded grades. "At that time, you were barely passing."

Roger frowned. "I wasn't trying hard then. My dad had a fit when that low grade report arrived in the mail."

"Well, your grades are improving. I've noticed that. You've been getting all of your assignments finished. No incompletes in the past two weeks."

"Eighty-three percent on a test is still just average. Not good for engineering school. My dad will take away my car privileges if I don't do better."

A wave of compassion washed over Karen. "Do you want to come in for extra help? I'm here most nights after school."

Roger sat a little straighter but looked at the floor. "Yeah, I guess so. I mean, I should."

"Which nights would work for you?"

"It would have to be Tuesday or Thursday. I have basketball practice the other three nights."

Karen dismissed thoughts of the times Roger had dropped pencils, made faces, and talked back. "How about Tuesdays?"

"I'd rather my dad didn't know about this. He's always telling me what a good student he was. All A's. Math was his favorite class. Honor Society. Scholarships. He wants me to be the same way." Roger sighed. "I'm not."

"I won't say anything to your dad unless he asks me. But surely, he'd want you to get extra help if you need it."

"No, you don't know my dad. He's a self-made man, and he expects the same from me. He doesn't listen to what I want. He tells me who he was and who I should be. His kid shouldn't need extra help, should be able to do everything on his own. Like he did. I've got to play basketball, too, like him. Always like him."

"How about your mom, Roger? Can you talk to her?"

"She's busy with her own life. Bridge club, hospital volunteer work, parties to help Dad's business, and stuff like that. Always going somewhere."

"I'll be here after school next Tuesday and the Tuesday after that. If you're interested, more Tuesdays could follow."

"I'll be here, Mrs. Antilla." Roger smiled. "By the way, about some of the stuff I did in class . . . You know . . ."

"I've already forgotten," Karen fibbed. "We're on a new page." That was the truth. From this day on, things should go much more smoothly in advanced algebra class.

Karen drove home thinking about the conversation with Roger. That's what teaching was all about, why she became a teacher in the first place. She loved math and working with kids, especially students with potential who needed to be inspired. Like Roger.

Her thoughts turned to her own son. She hadn't heard from Drew since the weekend he came home. She'd call him tonight. She hoped Drew had never felt pressured. *Thank God, Ari hadn't been like Roger's father.* Drew majored in business because he wanted to, not because he was coerced.

* * *

Karen was in such a good mood when she got home that she actually fixed a three-course meal for herself. A lettuce salad, minestrone soup, and a small steak. After cleaning up and putting the dishes in the dishwasher, she dialed Drew's number.

"Hi, Drew, haven't talked with you since you were home. How have you been?"

"Okay, Mom," he said in a monotone.

"How about your classes?" Right after she asked the question, she regretted it.

"Nothing new. I just keep plugging away."

"How about your Mustang? Is it running okay? It's getting up there in years."

"No problem."

She decided to bring up a pleasant topic. "I've got a little news. I told you about the boy in my algebra class who gave me some trouble. Do you remember?"

"Yeah, I do."

"He came to see me after school today. As a result, I'm going to give him extra help."

"I thought you said he wasn't interested in math."

"I did say that, but he seems to have lost his know-it-all attitude. He's going to try."

"That's good."

"He said his parents don't listen to him. I hope you never feel that way about me."

"No, Mom, I don't."

"That's a relief. After hearing him talk about his mother, I was a little worried. How's everything else there?"

"Oh, everything's the same, except I did go to see Jocelyn the other weekend. Took the train."

"That's a surprise. I haven't talked to her since she stormed out of the house. What's going on with her?"

"She's okay, still working at the same place."

"Drew, you sound groggy. Are you eating all right? Getting enough vitamin B?" She wanted to have an upbeat conversation with him, but his tone concerned her.

"Sure, Mom. You know me. I always take time to eat."

"Are you getting enough sleep?"

There was a long silence.

Karen spoke again. "I hope you're not studying so late or watching so much TV that you don't get your rest."

"No, it's not that, but I've had trouble falling asleep lately."

"Maybe you need more exercise, more fresh air."

"No, I don't think so. I'll be okay. I'm sure it'll pass."

She decided not to press the point. "How's Colin?"

"Oh, he's okay. He's around. I'm around. We don't talk much."

"Well, that's an interesting arrangement."

"I'm used to it. We go our separate ways." Drew paused. "I should get back to studying."

"Well, I'll let you go then, son. Take care of yourself. Remember I love you. Give me a call soon."

"I'll do that, Mom. Promise."

CHAPTER 24

"*I promise you won't remember this in ten years,*" *he says. He puts his right hand on her belly when the contractions start, looks at the watch on his left arm to time them, the way they learned in childbirth class. His face is intense, but he smiles at her, wipes her brow with a cloth. It's eight o'clock in the morning. They've been at the hospital since 3:00* AM.

Ari is the calm one when her water breaks.

"*It won't be long,*" *the doctor says.* "*Noon,*" *he predicts. Noon comes. No baby. Two o'clock. Four o'clock. She's very tired, too tired. She wants to sleep.*

"*You must stay alert,*" *he says.* "*Can't let a contraction get ahead.*"

The doctor says the baby is big, turning the wrong way in the birth canal. Seven o'clock. Eight. At last, the delivery room.

"*Push,*" *says the doctor.* "*Push,*" *says Ari, holding her from behind, lifting her back slightly.* "*Push,*" *says the nurse. Push, push, push. Nothing.*

They attach an oxygen mask to her face. She is afraid. Afraid for her baby. It's been too long. Please, God, my baby.

"*It will be fine,*" *he says.* "*I'm here. I'll always be here.*"

Push, push, push again. Yes. Ari holds. She pushes. Nurse pushes. Doctor pulls. First the head. "*A blond,*" *they say. Push more. Now the shoulders.*

"*It's a boy,*" *they say. Ari cries. She cries. Happy tears.*

I wanted a boy, she thinks, knowing it for the first time. Not just a healthy baby. A boy.

"Yes," says the doctor. "Your son is fine. Eight pounds, exactly."
Exactly!
Ari laughs. "He'll be a mathematician like his mama," he says.
"No, a stockbroker like his daddy," she says.
And the whole room fills with laughter.

Chapter 25

Karen hesitated outside the conference room of the Unitarian Church, not sure what to expect. She opened the door to a woodsy fragrance that reminded her of fresh forest greens. Several people chatted as they lounged on the upholstered chairs set in a circle around a square coffee table. Aha, there on the table was the source of the smell—a candle in a glass jar, burning silently next to a plate of cookies.

The room was softly lit. Karen appreciated the tall windows on two sides of the room although she couldn't see through them in the dark. All conversation stopped as the door clicked shut behind her. Two men and a number of women stared at her expectantly.

She cleared her throat. "Hi. Is there a Roberta Styles here?"

A young-looking woman with short striking salt-and-pepper hair stood, a feathery smile on her face. "I'm Roberta," she said, extending her hand. "You must be Karen. Glad you decided to come."

Roberta's approachable dark eyes peeked out from under delicate eyebrows, and her handshake was warm.

"We're just about to begin," she said. "Why don't you sit here?" Roberta patted the empty chair on her left.

As soon as Karen settled in, Roberta turned to the rest of the group. "Let's take a moment to introduce ourselves." She turned to the woman on her right. "Alondra, why don't you begin?"

Karen estimated the woman was in her early thirties.

"Hi. I'm Alondra," she said, brushing her long dark hair back from thin shoulders. She was fragile looking, her only makeup a modest layer of shimmery gloss applied to her lips. "My husband is gay, but he doesn't want a divorce. I'm trying to figure out what I should do." Alondra slumped back in her chair.

The tall blue-jeaned man to the right of Alondra spoke next. "I'm Tom," he said affably. His dark hair was short and curly and not particularly stylish, but his brown eyes emanated kindness. "My wife left with her girlfriend two months ago. I think she's just experimenting. I'm waiting for the novelty to wear off. I want her to come back."

Karen observed looks passing between several in the group as he spoke.

"My husband of fifteen years divorced me," said the next member of the group, who introduced herself as Melissa. A mountain of wavy blonde hair draped loosely over a soft sweatshirt that matched her lively blue eyes. "He had affairs with men for years before I knew. I knocked myself out trying to be a good wife and lover, but it didn't work. I thought there was something wrong with me, but now I know different." She stopped speaking for a moment before remembering something. "Oh, help yourself to the cookies I brought. Fresh baked. Coconut macaroon with chocolate chips."

"Oh, yum. Thanks," said Karen. She leaned across the table to select a cookie. Melissa was vivacious and pretty but a little on the chunky side. Karen guessed the roomy sweatshirt was Melissa's attempt to hide her weight, a ploy she understood well.

Karen sampled the cookie. "Delicious," she said, smiling in approval at Melissa.

Lucille, a short wiry dark-skinned woman, had gold-highlighted thick black hair that she'd pulled back off her face a short distance, secured with combs, then allowed to burst into a shower of spiky sprizzles. Stylish in a taupe pantsuit with a lacy camisole underneath, she spoke so fast that Karen had a hard time following.

"My husband met another man on the Internet," she said, not making eye contact with anyone. "I thought he was using the computer for business. Ha. He says he's going to move out as soon as they find a place. We have three kids. What on earth am I going to tell them?"

Karen understood the bitterness only too well. She felt sorry for Lucille's children.

The remaining member of the group, to Karen's immediate left, spoke. "I'm Baxter," he said, peering at her over bifocals that slid down his nose. "My wife wants to stay married but keep her girlfriend too." He rolled his eyes. "I don't know if I can accept that. I'm trying to figure out just what went wrong. I still love her, and she says she loves me even though she hasn't wanted to make love in a while. She suggested I come to this group."

Baxter was a balding, friendly sort. Karen could picture him barbecuing for crowds of friends and neighbors in a suburban backyard somewhere.

"Thanks, everyone," Roberta said. "Any announcements before we begin?"

Karen shifted uncomfortably in her chair. "I have something I want to say. My husband died more than two years ago, and from what I've heard, everyone else's spouse or former spouse is still alive. I really don't know if I belong in this group."

"Karen," said Roberta, "if you're here, trust that you belong. This is a safe place for you to express yourself. I don't think there's an issue you can address that someone hasn't been through. There's a code of confidentiality here, too. What is said stays in this room."

The anxiety in Karen's shoulders subsided. She was glad the difference she perceived was out in the open and that Roberta thought she belonged. She liked the idea of a place where she could express her feelings.

"All right, let's begin tonight's session talking about anger, an emotion most of you find yourself living with each day." She turned to Karen in explanation. "We spend some time each meeting talking about issues common to everyone."

Roberta addressed the group again. "Who'd like to begin?"

"Anger!" Melissa exploded from the other side of the circle. "I could talk for an hour. Look at me." She tugged at her sweatshirt. "I escaped into food. I'm angry this happened to me. Angry I couldn't see he was gay before I married him. Angry he didn't tell me. Angry he fooled around when I thought he was working nights." Melissa's voice rose with each declaration. "And right now most of all, I'm angry that my husband continued to have unprotected sex with me while he was fucking men. Shit. Now I have to be checked for HIV every six months. Anger, it rises in me like a volcano!"

Karen fell back, stunned by the punch of Melissa's words. Someone else with the same feelings. She, too, had had an AIDS test even though Ari had assured her that neither he nor Adrian was HIV positive.

Alondra edged forward, looked at Roberta, then asked hesitantly, "Can I talk about my anger?"

"Go ahead, Alondra, jump in."

Alondra twisted her wedding ring as she spoke. "The rest of the group knows this, Karen, but my husband told me six months ago he'd been having fantasies about other men. For years. That was hard, but I could accept it. Then two months ago, he told me he acted on his fantasy. He went to a gay bar one night after work. He danced. He . . . I don't know what all he did. But damn, I told him I could accept his fantasy, but he didn't have to do it, did he? He tells me he still loves me, wants to stay with me. I love him too, but what he did wasn't right. He's a married man. How could he do this to me?" She covered her face with her hands.

Roberta leaned over to touch Alondra's arm. "I know, Alondra. We all understand the feeling of betrayal here."

Everyone nodded, and the room fell silent. Alondra's hands dropped to her lap, and she stared at the floor.

To her own surprise, Karen began to speak. "We were married twenty years. I loved him. I thought he loved me. We had two children. I thought everything was good, but he definitely betrayed me. He met a man, led a double life. He loved him more than me." She drew in a sharp breath. "I don't know if he would have told me if it hadn't been for the cancer. Maybe it would have been better if I didn't know. I'm angry because he betrayed me. Angry because he told me. And angry because . . ." Karen's body shook as she burst sobs. "Because he died."

Roberta produced a packet of tissues from her purse, which she handed to Karen.

"Look at it this way," Lucille blurted, eyes blazing. "At least you don't have to listen to the lying bastard's excuses."

Karen stopped crying. Everyone sat in an astonished silence. Lucille's lack of tact was so absurd that Karen burst out laughing in spite of herself. "I like how you think," she said to Lucille. "And you're right, that's probably an advantage," she admitted.

The tension in the room eased. Karen dabbed the last of her tears away. "We used to make love a lot, but that changed. I thought it was me. I thought I was too fat. Too old. Not sensual enough. I thought I must be doing something wrong. He'd say, 'I'm tired, maybe this weekend.' But the weekend would come and nothing. He either forgot or busied himself with other things. Or there was a good movie on TV. And when we did have sex, well, it wasn't the same. The passion was gone. I blamed myself. He said I was beautiful, but it was only words. His arms were stiff when he hugged me, and his lips . . . I hate that he was gay and what he did to me."

"I've felt the same way," said Melissa.

Alondra nodded sadly. "Me too."

"I think we all have," Lucille added, her voice slow for a change. She glanced down at herself. "I used to think I was a hot babe. Now I feel invisible."

"It's not any different for men," Tom chimed in. "My wife pushed me away too."

"Well, my wife was willing to do anything I wanted," said Baxter. "Except I couldn't satisfy her. I didn't figure out why until it was too late."

Melissa shook her head. "The reality is you can't do anything to compete with your spouse's same-sex partner. Their yearnings have nothing to do with you."

"That is so very true," agreed Roberta, "and precisely what we need to tell ourselves. Every one of us."

Looking directly at Karen, Roberta continued, "Often people in this group find the emotions they feel are felt by others. It helps to find out you're not alone."

Everyone nodded in agreement, and the group continued to share for the next hour.

"It's good to acknowledge all of our emotions," Roberta said as the meeting concluded. "Pain. Depression. The trauma of finding out. Anger. Betrayal. Doubts about sexual attractiveness. Knowing that nothing will be the same again. Good session tonight, everyone. Have a good week, and we'll see you all next Thursday." She put the lid on the candle.

*   *   *

Melissa caught up to Karen in the parking lot. "Glad you joined the group, Karen. I know it was hard for you to come. It was for me, anyway. But I'm getting a lot out of it, and I hope you will too."

"Thanks, Melissa." Karen's step felt lighter on the way to her car as though she'd just kicked five pounds of mud from her shoes. To her amazement, she almost felt a flash of hope.

CHAPTER 26

*H*e flashes his contagious smile across the lawn. She can't help admiring his good looks. Sturdy, athletic build with firm, lean muscles, flat belly. Golden-flecked green eyes, white even teeth, golden-red hair. From his name, some assume Ari is Greek. But he's Finnish. Wholesome. Scandinavian. Even after six years, she can't believe he chose her.

She brushes her curls from her face, smiles back, then returns to pruning her roses, a passion handed down from her parents, both gone now.

He mows the lawn. Four-year-old Drew helps with his dull-bladed trimming shears, fashioned by his dad. Drew, eager to please. Drew, solemn, doing his job.

Three-year-old Jocelyn frolics on the lawn, singing, turning somersaults. "Look at me, Mommy, Daddy."

Karen smiles, at ease on this Saturday, working in her yard. Almost two years in this house. Such a change from New York City. She was never a city girl after all. Life is good.

CHAPTER 27

Adrian pulled his headset off in the windowless room and set it on the round boardroom table in front of him. "Great job, Patricia. You give a dynamite interview." He leaned back in his chair to study the slightly flushed woman at the microphone on the other side of the table.

Her fingers betrayed her uneasiness, alternating between twisting her rings and touching her stylish but tousled reddish blond hair. As nervous as Patricia seemed, when she smiled at Adrian, the corners of her soft brown eyes crinkled in kindness. She looked like a happily married mother from the suburbs. Adrian shook his head. Who would have guessed she'd fallen in love and run off with a woman at age forty-nine, leaving behind her husband, a financially secure life, and the country club?

"Thanks, Adrian. I'm not sure what I said. I just talked. I hope you find it useful."

"I'll definitely use this interview, Patricia. You spoke from the heart. Your courage amazes me."

Patricia's cheeks turned even redder than they already were. "I have to live my life truthfully, whatever it takes. Pardon me, but do you mind if I ask you a question?"

Adrian glanced at his watch. "Sure. We don't have to be out of here for half an hour. Go ahead."

"I just wondered, this is not your usual subject, is it? I mean, I've only heard you do Wall Street pieces before."

Adrian loosened his tie. "I used to do more variety, but you're right. In recent years, I've concentrated on the stock market and economic issues. This is a special project, one I requested. The station's going out on a limb to let me do it."

Patricia narrowed her eyes. "Is there a personal reason?"

"Yes, you might say that." Adrian smiled at her. "I don't usually mention this, but I'm gay too."

"I'd assumed that."

Adrian continued. "Unlike you, though, I've always known. Men and women who don't understand their orientation until middle age interest me because by then, life can be very complicated."

"No kidding," Patricia said, eyebrows arched. "My life was complicated, but I adjusted. Everyone adjusted."

Adrian nodded. "From what I've read, women are more apt to make quick life-changing decisions than men."

"Is that so?" Patricia leaned back. "I didn't know that. I assume you've interviewed men in this situation too."

"Yes." Adrian broke eye contact for a moment. "Actually, I have firsthand knowledge of a particular man."

"Oh," said Patricia softly, her eyes scrunched in concern. "I gather it didn't work out."

"For a time, it worked very well, even though he stayed with his wife. Our relationship ended when he died of cancer, more than two years ago."

"I'm sorry." Patricia looked at her hands and began to twist her rings again. Looking up, she asked, "How did you meet him? I mean, as a married man, he wasn't looking for a relationship, was he? I know I wasn't."

Adrian fixed his eyes on the control panel next to him. "I met him right here, in this studio. He was a stockbroker. I can't explain it. We just clicked, same sense of humor, same interests. Running, golf, Broadway plays, movies, books."

"Did you both recognize the attraction right away?"

"I knew instantly," said Adrian. "But I never guessed it went both ways. I knew he was married, and I assumed he wanted to keep it that way. But he was alone two or three nights a week here in the city, not far from my apartment. We started getting together. For dinner or a play or a drink. Then one night, we both had too much wine." Adrian felt his throat constrict. He was unable to continue.

"And then he knew too," said Patricia, finishing for him. "Like I knew."

"Yes, exactly." Adrian was grateful he didn't have to say the words. "But, as I said, he never left his wife."

"Why not?"

"Because she was a good woman, and they'd shared so much together. Two children. A beautiful home. Years of decisions and history. He loathed deceiving her."

"How often did you see each other?"

"Every night he was in town. At my place. The phone was a little tricky. He had his calls forwarded."

"It must have been hard, being so in love and seeing him so little. Knowing that you could never hope for more than you had."

Adrian studied her carefully. "Yes, that was hard, but I tried to live in the present, enjoy every moment we had. I didn't allow myself to think ahead. Otherwise, I wouldn't have had him at all."

"How long before the cancer?"

"Four years."

"I hope I'm not being too nosy."

Adrian smiled at her. "It seems we've reversed roles. You've become the interviewer. I'm generally a private person, but I don't mind talking to you. You're a good listener."

"It's interesting, listening from the other side. My lover went through what you did for a time. But we resolved it differently, and in your case, the man you loved died, so you can't say what would've happened. That makes it all the more tragic."

"Yes," said Adrian slowly. "Not only for me, but for his wife. She learned her husband was gay only a short time before he died. I know she didn't understand her husband's dilemma. Most people don't. That's why I want to do this piece."

"For her?"

"No, but for people like her."

"Because?"

"Because men and women discovering a different sexual identity at midlife are not as unusual as most would think. I want the pain and predicament on both sides to be understood."

"Have you ever had a conversation with her?"

Adrian shook his head. "No, not really. But that day is coming."

CHAPTER 28

Karen looked forward to her group each week. What a difference from despondency and isolation she'd felt the last few months when she'd kept her twice-monthly appointments with Margaret. Even though she saw the other members of the group only once a week, she often found herself thinking of each of them at different times. She couldn't put on a sweatshirt without thinking about Melissa, and when she saw a mother with young children, she pictured Lucille. She no longer felt quite so alone.

Roberta looked at her watch. "Time to start. Glad to see everyone here. Tonight, we're going to begin by talking about the things in our lives that have changed, or perhaps have been squashed and forgotten. What activities meant something to you when your relationship was good? What are the things that used to make you happy?"

"Oh, that's not hard," Melissa began. "We used to go into New York City three or four times a year to visit the art museums and galleries and to shop. I used to love shopping and wearing beautiful clothes. Ha, now I can hardly find a pair of pants that fit. Jack and I used to enjoy biking too, every Saturday afternoon in spring and summer. Until he got too busy with work, or so he said."

Tom jumped into the discussion. "Well, what's stopping you from getting your bike out?"

"Nothing, I suppose. But I don't have anyone to ride with now. And I'm so damned fat I hate to get on the bike."

"You remember biking with Jack as fun." Roberta paused. "Perhaps you could find a way to enjoy it again. With a friend?"

"And if you're thinking about your weight, biking could be a way to work on that," Karen contributed. "Not that I'm a good one to talk about weight," she laughed.

Baxter sat straighter in his seat. "You know, it's hard to think of things we enjoyed doing. I worked long hours managing the store. Now I could kick myself for that. I wasn't around for my wife. She had a lot of time alone."

"You can't blame yourself," Tom said. "You aren't responsible for your wife's decisions."

Roberta looked thoughtful. "But, Baxter, what did the two of you do together when you had time? Even before you were married? Or what did you enjoy doing alone?"

"Good question. Well, we went to movies, went out to eat, but we didn't socialize much with other couples. My work schedule was too tough for that."

Alondra added, "Your wife's life sounds like my life. No time for socializing because of my husband's long hours. What a bummer, I thought. I hadn't realized he spent some of those late hours at the bars. But I'm not up for a divorce."

Karen found herself sympathizing with Baxter's wife. It really didn't sound like he was around much. Still, cheating on him wasn't right.

Roberta continued, "Well, Baxter, you have to find something you're interested in. Something you enjoy doing by yourself or with other people. You have to reclaim your own identity somehow."

"But my wife isn't leaving," Baxter stated firmly.

"I realize that, Baxter. For now that's the way things are. You have to decide whether that works for you. Your wife will have to decide as time goes on whether that works for her too."

Karen spoke up. "Ari and I loved to dance. I used to fuss over my roses too. But now, I'm not interested in much of anything."

Alondra's eyes widened. "Dancing? What kind of dancing?"

"When I was a child, I took ballet." Karen smiled, her eyes glowing. "I went to lessons for years. As long as I can remember, I liked to dance."

"Was your husband a good dancer?" asked Lucille.

"Oh yes, he was magnificent. When we were both in college, we went to dances. And later, when we were newlyweds, we danced at home by candlelight." She sighed deeply. "And we were the couple to watch at weddings. Ari always had women clambering to be his partner."

"When was the last time you danced?" asked Alondra.

"It must be three years ago now." Karen sighed again.

"Well," Roberta commented, "going to dances or taking community dancing lessons is one way of meeting people."

"Oh, I couldn't do that. Look at me. I've gained so much weight since those days. I don't dance at all any more."

Melissa jumped in, a bright smile on her face. "Well, if I can ride my bike with all this weight, you can dance. Maybe you should bike with me, and I can take dance lessons with you."

Roberta chuckled. "Not a bad idea, Melissa. Karen, if dancing was important to you once, it can be again. It's up to you to find out how. And how about your flowers?"

"I used to grow beautiful roses . . ."

*   *   *

"Before we leave tonight," Roberta said, "something I want each of you to think about is, if your dream is gone, you can create another dream. If life the way it was is over, you can find a way to move on. But you don't have to abandon your past. You can each rediscover some of the things from the past that used to give you joy. The things you've talked about tonight."

Lucille spoke up. "Well, that might be easier for other people than for me. We have three kids. My life is taking care of them. I haven't had time for my own interests since the oldest was born eight years ago. The younger ones are five and three."

Tom said, "You can't make excuses, Lucille. That won't help."

"But, Tom, they won't understand if their father leaves. And I dread that he'll want to have them over on weekends. With this Internet guy. If it works out. I keep holding out hope that it won't."

Roberta looked directly into Lucille's eyes. "Lucille, it may or may not. That's out of your control right now. But you do have to find a way to move on. Become active at the kids' school. Join a church organization. Find a parenting class. Something."

Melissa said, "Don't be naive. Prepare yourself now for *when* your husband moves out."

"*If* he moves out," Lucille said fervently.

Melissa spoke again. "Yes, of course, if he moves out."

"My children are older," Karen shared. "My daughter had an easier time with it than my son."

"How do you know that?" asked Baxter.

"Well, my daughter is a person who can always bounce back. Outgoing. Popular. Much like her father. She understood. Didn't like it but understood."

"Didn't like what?" Roberta asked. "That he was gay?"

Karen squirmed. "Oh, I wouldn't say that. In fact, just recently she told me she's a lesbian and has known for a long time."

"What didn't she like?" asked Alondra.

"How everything changed. How our family changed."

"Did she say that in words, Karen?" asked Roberta.

"Not in words, but I know she didn't like what her father did to our family. I could sense it."

"And how do you feel about her being a lesbian?" Tom was nothing if not direct.

"We had strong words when she told me. I was furious, and she stomped out of the house. Several weeks ago. She didn't mince words. Ha! You can't imagine . . ." Karen's voice trailed off as she shook her head. "I wonder if her father had some influence on this, whether his being gay had an effect on her."

Roberta addressed Karen's comment. "Studies don't show any connection. If a parent is gay, a child is not any more likely to be gay than if both parents are straight."

"Well, how do you explain it?" Karen asked in exasperation.

Roberta looked Karen in the eye. "You don't," she said flatly.

"How's she doing now?" Lucille asked. "Have you talked to her since the blowup?"

Karen bit her lip. "No, I haven't. She owes me an apology."

"Someone has to take the first step," said Roberta. "The longer you wait, the harder it is." She paused before continuing. "And what about your son? How did he take the news of his father's gayness?"

"I'm not sure how he feels. He acts like he's in a fog. It's hard to tell whether he is in mourning or reacting to Ari's gayness, or both."

Roberta asked, "And how do you feel, Karen?"

"Sometimes I've wondered if my marriage to Ari was one big mistake, considering what each of us in the family is doing now. But other times, like today, when I look back and remember the good times, I don't think it was."

CHAPTER 29

*S*he enters the revolving door, and a tall woman brushes past. Her slow pace stands out in the city that hustles. She scrunches her eyes to read the wall, spots the sign for the elevator that will express her to the top.

Doors close. The tall woman again. Karen smiles.

The tall woman returns an unblinking blue-eyed stare, raises her chin, turns in dismissal. The woman's suit is form-fitting, leather. She is thin. Her sandy-colored hair is deliberately mussed. Pencil-thin eyebrows. High heels. Long, perfectly manicured fingernails. Expensive shoes and handbag match. And a pouty mouth coated in lipstick the color of grape sherbet.

Her tongue slides over her own uncoated lower lip. She glances at her well-worn handbag, sturdy shoes, and short unpolished nails.

She steps off the elevator and is confused. A man in a dark suit notices, asks her if she is looking for the restaurant.

"Yes, but first, the ladies room?"

She goes straight to the mirror, sets her purse on the ledge, fumbles with the contents. She finds a lipstick, carefully outlines with the brownish-rose hue. Next, she takes a small brush, bends at the waist, brushes her hair from the underside. She stands up, shakes it into place. Her medium-length dark tresses look exactly the same.

She turns sideways, studies herself in the mirror, runs her hands over her plump body, tugs at the bottom of her blouse. No hope. She returns the brush and lipstick to her purse and walks out the door.

He sees her, sets down his martini glass, rises to his feet. He grins, but there is no mirth in his smile. Even so, she can't help but admire how handsome he looks in his perfectly tailored gray suit. But today, he looks extremely fatigued.

She is afraid.

"What's wrong?" she asks.

"The tests are back," he replies. "It's bad, very bad. Cancer. Cancer of the pancreas. And it's probably too late."

Too late. Too late. Too late.

CHAPTER 30

Jocelyn awoke to the sound of a ringing telephone. She glanced at the clock on the nightstand as she reached for the receiver. Almost noon.

"Hello?"

"Jocelyn, it's me. Calling on my lunch hour."

She recognized her mother's voice and felt a wave of dread. "Hey, Mom. Just woke up. Worked late last night." She yawned as if trying to prove her words.

"Yes, you're hard to catch. Normally I don't make calls on my lunch hour. But we haven't talked for so long."

Jocelyn coughed. "Yes, well. Didn't think you particularly wanted to talk to me."

"Now, that's where you're wrong, Jocelyn. Nothing means more to me than my kids. Even if we don't agree, I'm still your mother."

Jocelyn was at a loss for words. She couldn't read her mother this time. Was she trying to make her feel guilty?

"Jocelyn, are you still there?"

"Yes, Mom. Just thinking. So you're not mad at me anymore?" She pushed the covers aside and perched on the edge of the bed.

"No, I'm not. I'm sorry I upset you the last time you were home. I said some things I shouldn't have."

The shield protecting Jocelyn's heart lowered a little. "I said some things too, Mom. I'm sorry. But, just so you know, I meant most of what I said. Even though I know I shouldn't have gone ballistic."

"That's okay. Let's not dwell on it, dear. Let's move on and try as best we can to work out our differences."

"Mom, you sound . . ." Jocelyn hesitated. "You sound . . . calmer. And not so . . . down."

"I guess that's a good thing. Actually, I think what you say is true. I've been doing something different. For one thing, I've stopped seeing Margaret."

"Oh, Mom, no therapist? Do you think that's wise?"

"I didn't say no therapist, honey. I'm seeing a new one but as part of a group. On Thursday nights. I've gone four times now, and it's good. Helping me to see things in a different perspective."

"Well, whatever it is, Mom, if you feel better, I'm glad."

"Thanks, dear. Now, what about you? What's going on in your life?"

Again, Jocelyn was hard-pressed to find words. What could she possibly say to her mother about her life at present? She was certain her mom wouldn't want to hear about Lisa, nor could she talk about her visits with Adrian. Other than that, there wasn't much going on except work. Ah work. There was something.

"Oh, I'm pretty busy with work, Mom. But here's something you'll be glad to hear. Someone loaned me a book, and it's been quite interesting. I've been trying to figure out a career. Haven't thought of anything specific yet, but I know I don't want to waitress forever."

"That *is* good news, dear. What sort of occupations might you consider?"

"Don't know for sure. Something physical. Something where I can help people. I met a physical therapist, and that sounds like an interesting career, one I'd like. But . . . it's so hard to get into that field. You practically have to be top of the class, and then they only take a few candidates each year. I don't think I've got it in me to work that hard to try to qualify and maybe end up not being able to get in, anyway. So I'm trying to think of something else."

"Sounds like you're on the right track. If there's any way I can help you with these decisions . . ."

"Yes, Mom, I'll be sure to ask for advice if I need any. Thanks."

"How are you doing financially? You haven't asked for anything extra from your trust lately."

Oh, the trust, Jocelyn thought cynically. Money from her mom's parents, guarded by her mom. "I'm doing okay. Nothing leftover, that's for sure, but tips are good, and that helps the ends meet."

"Let me know if you get in a tight spot, all right?"

"Sure, Mom. I'll do that. Hope I don't have to, though." She could hear her mother chuckle on the other end of the phone.

"Yes dear," Karen said. "I know how independent you are."

It gave Jocelyn a warm feeling to hear her mother laugh even if it was just a little. "I'm glad you called, Mom."

"I'm glad I did too, Jocelyn. But I've got to go in just a moment. Wish you could get home more often, but I know you never get a full day off on the weekend. Do you?"

Jocelyn winced, wondering whether she should lie. "Well, as a matter of fact, I'm off this Saturday. But I couldn't possibly come home. Not this time. I've just got too much to do here. You know, cleaning the place. I'm really behind. And I'm up to my ears in laundry. But another time, Mom. Soon."

"Oh, that's too bad. Wish you could have come. But I, of all people, certainly know what it's like to have to catch up with the house on days off. Well, I've got to go, sweetie. Love you."

"Love you, too, Mom. Bye now."

CHAPTER 31

She remembers that Sunday in September when she still had hope. Kids both away at college, she and Ari are alone. Ari is tired, in the early stages of treatment, sleeps on the sofa in front of the fire, wrapped in a blanket.

She takes off her clothes, sneaks under his blanket, nestles into his body. He awakes, smiles at her. She kisses him. He kisses her back, but no more. She pushes her breasts toward him, but he doesn't touch. Hasn't touched for a long time now. She wonders how long it's been.

"Why?" she asks aloud.

"Why what?" he answers.

"Why don't we make love any more?"

He looks at her a long time, doesn't answer. She sees pain in his eyes. Then tears. She thinks he will tell her it's because he's too tired, because he's been tired a long time, a lot longer than he's been sick. She thinks he will tell her they're too busy, or they're too old, or it'll be better next year. But he doesn't speak. The air is pregnant with the words he cannot say.

She is afraid now. The longer he is silent, the more afraid she becomes.

Finally, he begins to speak, but he looks away from her as tears begin to flow down his face.

Slowly he tells her the reason. "It's because . . . because . . . I'm gay."

First, she hears nothing but the silence. Then she hears another woman, not her, but someone else who must be in the room. The other woman is screaming, "Nooooo!"

She looks around but sees no other woman in the room. How could she make that sound and not know?

"Karen, there's more," he says.

How can there be more, she thinks. Isn't that enough?

"Karen," he continues, "I have a lover. A man I've been seeing for some time now. I haven't been able to tell you, haven't wanted to tell you. You're such a good person, Karen. You don't deserve this."

"Stop!" the other woman screams. "I can't be hearing this. I don't want to hear this. Don't tell me how good I am when you're fucking someone else!"

"Oh, Karen. I didn't want this."

He cries, she cries, they hold each other. Until dark. Until dark, but not death.

CHAPTER 32

Adrian watched as Jocelyn set up to hit her drive on the eighteenth tee, her head tilted slightly to the right as she shuffled her feet to find just the right position. She waggled the club behind the ball three times, pressed her wrists forward slightly, then drew the club back. Her knees changed direction first, then her legs, and finally, her arms.

The shaft of the club whistled as it whipped through the air just before the clubhead smacked the ball straight and long down the fairway. She finished facing her target with arms over her left shoulder, weight on her left foot.

Even if Adrian hadn't seen the flight of the ball, that telltale tongue dangling over her lower lip would have told him she'd made a great shot.

Adrian smiled. Ari had taught his daughter well. She was almost as good as he had been.

"Nice shot, Jocelyn. Looks like you outdrove me."

"Thanks. We were even going into this hole, right?"

"Right. We're tied. Four hours of play, and it comes down to the final hole."

They tossed their bags over their shoulders and headed down the fairway, enjoying the Saturday afternoon sunshine. When they reached Adrian's ball, Jocelyn removed her bag from her shoulder and rummaged for a snack.

"Want an apple? Think I've got two," she said as she continued to dig in a pocket.

"No thanks, but if you're hungry, I'd be delighted to buy you a hamburger or whatever at the clubhouse when we finish."

Jocelyn smiled gratefully. "Thanks, but I have to pass." She looked at her watch. "Lisa's coming over tonight. Anyway, you'd better hit your shot if you want to beat me." She took a large chomp out of her apple. Scrumptious. Just the right combination of tart and sweet.

Adrian chuckled. "Always the competitor, aren't you?"

"Yup." Another chomp.

Adrian's ball missed the green in favor of a sand trap. Jocelyn's shot landed at the front of the green and snaked its way toward the hole at the back, stopping only two feet short.

"I surrender. I can feel my two dollars leaving my wallet already!"

"Well, you never know. You could put that sand shot right in the hole. It's happened before."

"Who do you think I am, kiddo? Tiger Woods?"

"Oh, stop whining," Jocelyn's voice was gleeful. "Accept your fate graciously!"

"Hey, do you want a ride home or not?"

Adrian made an outstanding shot from the greenside bunker, putting the ball about five feet from the hole and making the putt. But Jocelyn easily made her two-footer, winning the contest.

"Good game, Jocelyn. I don't mind losing to such a fine player, a woman no less, playing from the same tees I am. Shall we head for the parking lot?"

"A woman no less?" she punched his arm playfully. "Hey, this has been great. I've missed getting out here."

"We'll have to do this more often. Does Lisa play golf?"

"A little bit, I guess. We've never been out on a course, so I don't know for sure how she plays. I'll have to find out."

They placed their clubs in the trunk of Adrian's black Audi and climbed into the front.

"So, how's it going with Lisa?"

Jocelyn's face lit up. "Terrific! We like so many of the same things—music, movies. We both love *Dirty Dancing*, watched that last week." She smiled, apparently remembering something. "And we even laugh at the same things."

"You both like to dance, I gather?"

She looked at him in surprise. "Yeah, how'd you know?"

"Oh, your dad was quite the dancer. And I heard your mom was too."

"Yes. They were both great. Now that I think of it, I remember them dancing around the living room when I was a little kid, looking like Patrick Swayze and Jennifer Grey in that movie. They were hot. Especially Mom."

Adrian returned to the subject. "How many dates have you had with Lisa?"

"Oh, probably about six." She paused to look sideways at Adrian. "We haven't, you know . . . done anything. Besides kissing and hugging, I mean."

Adrian laughed. "I wasn't asking, was I?"

"No, I guess you weren't. I guess maybe I just wanted to tell you."

"Are you disappointed that your relationship hasn't gone further?"

"Oh no. Maybe. Well, yes, I guess I am. I'm caught between wanting it real bad and feeling like if we do, I'll be so inadequate. No experience, you know. But oh god. The feelings I have when our bodies press together."

Adrian grinned. "Don't worry. You'll be fine."

*   *   *

They made good time on the freeway, pulling in front of Jocelyn's apartment complex forty minutes later.

As she reached for the door handle, Jocelyn remembered something. "Hey, Adrian, can you wait here a minute? I want to return that book you loaned me, on careers. I'm done with it."

"Look, there's a parking spot right here if you can believe it. Why don't I park and walk up with you while you get the book? That way you'll have more time to get ready for your date."

"Sure."

Adrian maneuvered the Audi into the parking spot then opened the trunk to retrieve Jocelyn's golf clubs. They walked to the elevator, pushing the button for the third floor.

"You and Dad never met here, did you?" asked Jocelyn as she fished her key out of her golf bag outside the door.

"No. We always met at my place."

"Well, come in for a moment while I get the book."

"Sure." They walked into the apartment, first the entryway, then into the living room. Both stopped in their tracks at the sight of a woman sitting on the sofa.

Jocelyn dropped her golf clubs. "Mom!"

"Jocelyn! Thought I'd surprise you, but you weren't home so I let myself in and—oh my god!"

Jocelyn watched as the color of her mother's face changed from slightly pink to chalk white when she saw who was with her. "Mom, you remember Adrian," she stammered, "I mean, you recognize Adrian, don't you?"

Karen was too stunned to either speak or stand. She just stared at her daughter, both hands covering her mouth.

Adrian cleared his throat. "Hello, Karen. I'm sorry to surprise you like this. I was just dropping Jocelyn off. I can see I'm making you uncomfortable, so I'll leave now. Jocelyn, take care."

"No, Adrian, don't leave, I'll get the book . . ."

"Another time, Jocelyn." He smiled gently at her, hastily exiting the apartment.

CHAPTER 33

Shaking with anger, Jocelyn glared at her mother. "Mom, how dare you arrive unannounced."

Karen rose to her feet and glared back. "How dare *you* consort with that man, behind my back, in the apartment bought by my parents! Does he have no limits? First, he seduces your father, now you!"

Jocelyn's jaw dropped in astonishment. "For god's sake, Mom, Adrian's gay! What a ludicrous statement."

"Ludicrous? Let me tell you what's ludicrous, young lady—"

"Don't bother, Mom, I know the speech. Save it for someone who gives a shit. You had no right to barge in here without an invitation."

Karen threw up her hands in exasperation. "I intended to do a nice thing! You led me to believe you were going to be home doing nothing but housework. I thought I'd surprise you and take you out for a nice dinner and maybe a movie, damn it! How was I to know you were lying? If you'd just told me the truth, this never would have happened."

"Ya, Mom. Like I can tell you the truth."

Karen narrowed her eyes. "We're getting sidetracked. Just what, exactly, was Adrian doing here? That's what I want to know right now."

"We played a round of golf this afternoon. We've gone for walks once in a while since I moved to the city and played a few rounds of golf as well. No big deal."

Tears welled in Karen's eyes. "I feel violated. You're all in conspiracy against me. When and how did this . . ." she struggled for the word, "this relationship start? I assume Adrian contacted you at some point."

Jocelyn sighed. "I was the one to contact him. We'd talked some at the hospital. He's a nice man, Mom. You'd actually like him if you could have met him under other circumstances."

"I don't understand why you contacted him."

"I don't either, Mom. I needed to. You know, in everything he's ever said, he's always been supportive of you, sensitive to how you might feel. He's a class act."

The dam broke. A wall of tears rushed down Karen's face. "It sounds like you have a higher opinion of him than you do of me."

The tears annoyed Jocelyn. She didn't like being manipulated. "Mom, it's not a contest. You're my mother, but damn it, you haven't exactly been available for us since Dad died, for me or Drew."

"You haven't had a good word to say to me since the day your father died. First, I find out you're lesbian. Next, I find out your best friend is your dead father's lover. I'm sick to death of trying to deal with you."

"Then don't, Mom. It'll be fine with me!"

At that moment, the door buzzer sounded. They both stared at the intercom.

"Now what?" said Karen.

"Oh, god. It's Lisa. She's early."

"Lisa? Who's Lisa?"

Jocelyn scowled at her mother then walked over to the intercom.

"Lisa? Come on up." She pushed the button that would open the entry door then turned to her mother. "Lisa is my girlfriend, Mom. We have a date tonight. Here."

Karen looked wildly around the room. "Where's my purse? I've got to get out of here. I'm not ready for this."

"Too late, Mom."

Karen grabbed her coat, noticing her purse underneath it. "In any case, I'm leaving. Now. I certainly would not want to interrupt your day any more than I already have." Her voice reflected a mixture of sarcasm and hurt.

Sure enough, when Karen opened the door, she was face-to-face with Lisa who had her hand raised, ready to knock.

"Lisa, meet my mom," Jocelyn called out from behind.

Lisa extended her hand, but Karen did not take it. With tears in her eyes, she stumbled to the elevator.

CHAPTER 34

*D*amn, he'd failed the fucking test, Drew thought as he slammed the apartment door. He had a hard time concentrating, but damn, he did the best he could. He threw his backpack onto the couch, slumped beside it, turned on the TV, and used the remote to flip through channels. Maybe he'd find something to watch to get his mind off the exam. Imagine, an econ major flunking a test in business. Humiliating. He should have gone into social work. Then he could have helped screwed-up people in screwed-up situations, people like himself. Too late now.

Colin strolled out of his bedroom stretching and yawning. "Man, these late hours get to me once in a while. Didn't hear you come home. I'm going to fix a frozen pizza and have a beer. You want some?"

"No, I'm not hungry. Maybe later."

"Later the pizza will be gone. What's wrong with you, you dumb shit, you're racing through the channels like a rabbit with a shotgun on his ass. Can't you just find a program to watch?"

Drew continued to flip through television channels. "I had a rough day, all right?"

"What happened? Flunk a test or something? Another babe give you the brush?"

"Knock it off. It's none of your fucking business."

"Geeze, just trying to make small talk. You don't have to bite my head off. Sure, you don't want some pizza?"

"No pizza. But hey, do you still have that whisky from the last party?"

"Yeah, what if I do?"

"Mind if I have some?"

"Huh? You? In the afternoon? It's in the cupboard above the fridge."

"I just found out I flunked a test if you want to know."

"Dang. How'd you find out on a Saturday?"

"The old-fart professor posted the results as soon as he corrected the exams. I flunked. Flunked. Fucking flunked. Big fat fucking flunked failure."

"That's not good so close to graduation, man."

"Sure, rub it in." Drew went to the kitchen, found the whisky, and mixed himself a whisky and water. He plopped down again in front of the TV with his drink.

Colin came into the living room with a plateful of pizza. "Sure you don't want some?"

"Damn it, do you have to keep asking? I said no."

Colin ate piece after piece of pizza. "You know I'm going out with Grace tonight. She's not such a dog after all. We're studying history together, at her place. At least that's the plan for early in the evening."

"What the fuck do I care, man? I'm just minding my own business."

"Geeze, don't bite my head off. Enjoy your night." Colin finished his pizza and went out the door.

Drew poured himself another drink and tried to focus on the TV, but he couldn't concentrate. He flipped through the channels again and again. Nothing. Like his life. His father, gay. Shouldn't have married at all. His mother, if she'd married someone else, he would be someone else. Or he never would've been born. *What would it be like not to exist?* It couldn't be more painful than living with the feelings going through his head right now.

He walked to the kitchen for more whisky. His mother knew nothing about his life. If she did, he'd just disappoint her. He probably won't find a job after college if he graduates at all. Geeze, how had he flunked that test?

He poured another whisky and water then picked up the phone, fingering the buttons. No one to call. Who'd even want to hear from him? His mother? She'd probably talk about the same old crap again, and he didn't want to hear it. Jocelyn? She'd probably be out. He'd blown his chance with Grace. Damn, now Colin was over there with her. Studying. Ha. He put the receiver down. No one to call. Back to the TV. And another drink.

* * *

Drew roused from the sofa. Someone was pounding on the apartment door. "Colin, you home?" Drew didn't recognize the voice.

He yelled from the couch, "Colin's not home."

"What the fuck? Where is he, you know?"

"I don't know, and I don't care, damn it."

The voice persisted, "He borrowed my chemistry notes. I need 'em back."

"I said he's not here."

"Damn, let me in, I'll look around."

"Just go away."

"Asshole."

Drew heard the footsteps walk down the porch steps and the slam of a car door. The jerk was gone. He finished his drink, rolled over, and went back to sleep.

*   *   *

An hour later, Drew poured himself another drink. Straight whisky this time. His head began to whirl. If his mother saw him this way, she'd be shocked. He raised his glass to converse with it. "Hi, Mom. Yeah, it's me. The responsible one. The one who flunked. Date? What's that? I'm too busy getting drunk. You want to join me?"

Did his father drink with Adrian? *God, maybe if Dad had never met that man, the family would have had a normal life. He'd have died anyway, but it would've been different.*

The bottle was almost empty.

Maybe it was his mother's fault. Maybe she wasn't woman enough. No, that wasn't fair. All those happy times couldn't have been charades.

Seven o'clock. He'd just finish off the whisky and watch TV. God, his head was pounding. He reeled to the bathroom, feeling dizzy. He opened the medicine cabinet and spotted the brown bottle of sleeping pills. Maybe they would help.

On his way to the couch, he snagged a beer from the fridge, taking the pills with him.

Another Saturday night alone. He set the pill bottle on the table beside him. *What time was it now?* His watch said 8:01 PM. Misfit. Can't do anything right. Don't measure up. Flunked the test. Flunked with Grace. Flunked as a son.

He twisted the cap from the sleeping pills, counted them slowly one by one. Thirteen in all. They filled the palm of his hand. He studied them and put them back.

Drew gulped another beer, finishing it in a few swallows. The headache again. A few pills might take the splitting headache away. Away. He opened the bottle again, took them out one at a time. One. Two. Three. Four. He popped them into his mouth and swallowed. Away. What if he would just go away? Born. Not born. Not born. Just a few pills. Who was he anyway? He could see his mother giving a cold stare to his father. Why did they ever meet? It was all a big mistake.

He emptied the bottle of pills onto the couch, studied them, rolled them between his fingers. Maybe more pills would make him feel . . . maybe nothing at all.

He'd call his mother and let her know. First button. No answer. Answering machine. "Hi, Mom. Drew. S'not your fault. Love you." He hung up. His head didn't hurt so much anymore.

He pushed the button for Jocelyn's number. His head swirled. *Shit, no answer. Leave a message. Now. Before too late.* "Josey . . . Me . . . You . . . Shouldn' be . . ." The phone fell out of his hand and clattered to the floor.

CHAPTER 35

Startled, Lisa stood aside as Karen rushed past.

"Nice to meet you too," Lisa said in a bewildered voice. She turned to look at Jocelyn. "You okay?" She touched Jocelyn's cheek.

Jocelyn stood very still with her head lowered, not meeting Lisa's inquiring eyes.

Lisa took Jocelyn's hands in hers, crouched down, and peered into Jocelyn's face.

Jocelyn burst into tears. Wordlessly, Lisa gathered her in her arms and let her cry. Gradually the sobs subsided, and Jocelyn began to speak.

"This always happens. Just when things start to look good between us, one of us blows up, and we have another fight. Mom said I haven't spoken a kind word to her since Dad died, and she's right. I haven't."

"No? That doesn't sound like you, Jocelyn."

"I've tried to understand, Lisa, but I just can't forgive her for what she did . . . no, for what she *didn't* do at the end . . ."

"What do you mean?" Lisa asked.

Jocelyn took a deep breath and reached for the tissue box next to the sofa. "Can we talk about that later? Right now . . . I'd like to concentrate on something more pleasant . . . like you and me."

"I see." Lisa glanced sideways at Jocelyn with an impish grin. "Josey, why don't you sit on the floor, and I'll massage your neck and shoulders. Not many people would turn down an offer like this from a physical therapist, you know."

Jocelyn smiled. She liked that Lisa sometimes used Drew's name for her. It made her feel special.

"You're right, that's an offer I can't refuse. But, I have another idea."

"Yes?"

"How about . . . instead . . . you could give me a full body massage . . . in the bedroom?"

Lisa grinned widely. "Oh, I could be persuaded. With, or without?"

"With or without what?"

"Clothes, silly!"

Jocelyn blushed, noticing the heat, not in her face . . . but elsewhere.

"Without. Definitely without." She turned to face Lisa fully.

They kissed hungrily, their hands relentless as they roved each other's bodies, desperate to feel what was underneath. Hearts pounding, they rose from the sofa and went to the bedroom where they slowly took off each other's clothes.

Lisa playfully pushed Jocelyn onto her back and began kissing her neck, moving down until she reached Jocelyn's breasts. Cupping a breast with one hand, she licked and savored. The fingers of her other hand slid through the silken forest until they found the hot, wet crevice that they craved.

Jocelyn gasped and moaned in pleasure. Lisa knew exactly when and how to stroke, to excite, to please. She persisted until Jocelyn's virgin body went rigid, and she cried out in delicious ecstasy.

They clung to each other, not speaking. Lisa was the first to break the silence.

"How's that for a massage?"

"Oh, god! Lisa! I have only one thing to say . . ."

"Yes?"

"Lie back!" With a bravery that surprised her, she kissed Lisa the way Lisa had kissed her, sliding her hands over Lisa's body, hoping she'd be able to find the groove that Lisa had so easily found on her. She did. The inside of Lisa was slippery and beautiful, like a ripe, expectant avocado. Her fingers glided up and down, faster and faster, finding their own rhythm without any prompting. Jocelyn could feel Lisa's body pumping up, rising and building until she rose to the top, then fluttered down as gently as a free-falling feather.

"Jocelyn," Lisa gasped, "it isn't possible that you've never done this before!"

Jocelyn grinned. "I love you, Lisa. And not only have I never made love before . . . I've never told anyone I love them."

As they held each other tight, luxuriating in the feel of their bodies together, the phone rang.

"Leave it," Jocelyn commanded. "The answering machine in the living room will pick up. Not expecting any calls anyway."

In the distance, they could hear a voice droning for a short time, a clunk, then nothing. They looked at each other. Without words, they rose and dashed into the living room. The message recorder clicked off. Jocelyn pushed the Play button.

"Josey . . . Me . . . You . . . Shouldn' be . . ."

It was Drew! His words trailed off.

CHAPTER 36

Jocelyn's heart pounded hard in her chest. "Does he sound drunk to you? He's not making sense."

"Let's play it again," advised Lisa.

They played the message three more times before Lisa offered her opinion. "Yes, he does sound drunk. His words are definitely slurred. Why don't you call him back and see if he answers."

Jocelyn dialed Drew's number and heard a busy signal. "What should I do?" A wave of alarm rose in her throat, but before Lisa could answer, she had her own solution. "I know. I'll call the operator." She dialed the operator who confirmed the line was busy, but no one was talking.

Lisa looked on as Jocelyn dialed another number. "Who—"

"My mom," Jocelyn explained. "She's closer, and she'll know what to do. Damn, she's not home, I've got her answering machine."

She hung up without leaving a message then thought a moment. "Gotta do it," she mumbled as she picked up the phone again. "Please be home," she pleaded.

"Adrian! Thank God, you're there. Listen, I don't have time for details, but Drew called here, and I didn't answer the phone. He left a message on the machine though, which I heard right after. His speech was slurred, and he was starting to say something, but the phone dropped. Then nothing. His line is busy now, and the operator says there's no conversation on the line. I don't know what I should do. Don't want to get him in trouble if nothing's wrong, but I'm worried. I can't find Mom. What should I do?"

"Jocelyn, hang up and call 911 immediately," Adrian instructed. "Give them Drew's name and address. They'll ask for yours and a phone number. Give them my cell number. I'm on my way over right now in my car. Meet you in front. I'll be there as fast as I can."

The 911 operator connected her with the Hartford emergency services. While Jocelyn gave the dispatcher information, Lisa quickly dressed and retrieved Jocelyn's clothes, helping her into them as she juggled the telephone. After Jocelyn's jeans and shirt were on, Lisa pushed her onto the sofa to help her into her socks and shoes. By the time Jocelyn hung up, all she needed to run out the door was her coat.

"Come with me, Lisa," she pleaded as they took the elevator down.

"I don't know if I should, Josey. I don't want to be in the way during a critical family time like this."

"Well, *I* want you with me, okay?"

Adrian's Audi pulled up as they emerged from the building. Jocelyn ran to the curb as Adrian flung the passenger side door open from the driver's seat.

"Okay if Lisa comes too? I asked her if she would."

"Sure, get in. Hi, Lisa. I'm Adrian."

Jocelyn climbed into the front seat while Lisa got into the back of the spotless Audi. Adrian handed Jocelyn his cell phone and instructed her to keep trying her mother as they drove.

"Where could she have gone?" Jocelyn asked no one in particular. "I hope she's not wandering the city aimlessly. I know she was upset when she left, but I thought she was okay. God, I wish I'd answered the phone. I was right there."

"I don't know if it would have made much difference, Jocelyn," said Adrian. "You said he only spoke a couple of words before he dropped the phone. I think the same thing would have happened even if you'd answered."

Adrian is truly a gentleman, Jocelyn thought to herself. *Doesn't even ask why I didn't answer the phone.* She was quite certain her mother would have wanted an explanation. On that note, she dialed her mother again. Still no answer.

"Will the police or the paramedics or whoever actually break in? Or call us to let us know what's going on?"

"I don't know," said Adrian. "Why don't you call the Hartford police and ask them? They can direct us."

Jocelyn called the cell phone operator who connected her with the Hartford police immediately. She learned that Drew had been found unconscious and was being transported to Hartford Hospital.

"Thank you," said Jocelyn to the dispatcher. Grim-faced, she relayed the information to Adrian and Lisa.

"Unconscious!" exclaimed Lisa. "Do you suppose he tried to—" She stopped short, not wanting to voice the possibility.

"No! Damn it!" Jocelyn exploded. "It must be an accident. I know my brother. Sure he's been low lately, but he wouldn't . . . No, I just can't see it. Only thing that surprised me recently was that he was drinking . . . Oh, god. Do you suppose it's alcohol poisoning? Could he have—"

"We're nearing Stamford," Adrian said, cutting in. "Give your mom a try again, Jocelyn."

CHAPTER 37

When the train arrived in Stamford, Karen realized how hungry she was. The hot dog from the street vendor near Jocelyn's apartment had worn off. If all had gone as planned, she and her daughter would have been eating in a restaurant on Theater Row right now. But, no, Jocelyn's plan with her girlfriend put an end to that.

As she stepped off the train onto the platform, Karen decided she'd catch a quick bite. Maybe the Meadow Inn. She hadn't eaten there since she and Drew had gone out for breakfast.

Karen felt someone touch her arm as she walked to the parking lot. She turned. It was Melissa, her face beaming.

"Karen, hi. We must have been on the same train. Darn, if only I'd seen you earlier. It would have made the ride back from the city more enjoyable."

"Oh, hi, Melissa. Gosh, we must have been in different cars. So you went into the city today too?"

"Yes, I did. After group Thursday night, I decided to treat myself and visit the Metropolitan Museum of Art, something Jack and I always used to do. It wasn't quite the same going alone, but . . ."

"Say, Melissa, I was thinking of stopping at the Meadow Inn for a sandwich. Are you hungry?"

"Sure thing. I definitely wouldn't mind having something to eat. No reason to rush home either."

*   *   *

Mrs. Martin was positioned in her usual spot at the hostess stand. She spotted Karen instantly. "Well, Mrs. Antilla, haven't seen you in a while." She glanced at the two women. "Table for two tonight?"

"Yes, Mrs. Martin. Actually a booth, if possible."

"Sure thing. It's a busy night, but I still have one booth available. Follow me."

Mrs. Martin led Karen and Melissa to the booth.

* * *

"Melissa, I'm glad to have run into you. You know, after group Thursday night, I decided to telephone my daughter even though I'd said that I thought she owed me an apology."

"Good for you. I'm sure that wasn't easy to do."

"No, but I was glad I did it. We both did some apologizing for things we said the last time we talked. I was so heartened by the conversation that I decided to go into the city and surprise her with a visit today."

"So that's why you were in the city! Did you have a nice day?"

Karen rolled her eyes and tried to smile. "No, it turned out to be a nightmare. Do you have time for me to tell you about it? I'd like to hear about your day too."

"Yes, of course, I have time. Let's order first."

* * *

"Well, I can understand your disappointment, Karen. And what a shock to come face-to-face with both Adrian and your daughter's girlfriend on the same day."

Karen shook her head. "Melissa, I wasn't prepared. It was just too much. So unexpected. I couldn't deal with it today, and I wonder if I ever will be able to. I'll have to talk about this in group Thursday night." She wiped her eyes with a tissue.

"Karen, as I said to you in the parking lot the first night you came to the group, don't be so hard on yourself."

Karen stared across the table at place next to Melissa. Someone was in it. It couldn't be. She blinked. Ari, in a blue turtleneck!

"Are you all right, Karen?" asked Melissa. "You look pale."

Go home, Karen. There's trouble.

She saw his mouth move but heard his voice in her head. What was going on? Then as quickly as Ari had come, he vanished.

"Karen?" Melissa repeated.

"Oh, I'm sorry. It's been a long day. Ready to go? Let's just split the bill."

*   *   *

Karen entered her house, laid her coat over a chair, and slipped off her shoes. She was still shaken by the vision of Ari. Her answering machine was beeping. *There's trouble.* Her heart began to pound.

She pushed the Play button and listened to the message. "Hi, Mom. Drew. S'not your fault. Love you." *Oh my god, he sounds drunk. What time did that call come in? Eight twenty. An hour and twenty minutes ago.* There'd been five other calls, but no messages. One call from Jocelyn. Then four calls from an unknown cell phone, the last only ten minutes ago.

Drew, she had to phone Drew. She dialed his number. No answer. Frantic, she phoned Jocelyn's number. No answer. Why hadn't Jocelyn left a message?

As she stood there, the phone rang. She snatched the receiver. "Hello?"

"Mom, I've been trying to get you for an hour. Something's wrong with Drew. They've taken him to Hartford Hospital. He's unconscious. I'm in a car right outside of Stamford. We'll stop by and pick you up. Right away."

Karen shrieked, "Unconscious. No. Can't be. I just got home. He left a message on my machine. I tried to reach him."

"I know, Mom, he left a message for me too. I tried to call you. Then I called Adrian. Then 911. Adrian said he'd drive me to Hartford. Just a moment, Mom, I have to give Adrian some directions here . . ."

"Oh, my baby boy," Karen wailed. "I wasn't here for him when he needed me. He called me, and I wasn't home. God, please, God, let him be okay. Adrian? Oh no. Not Adrian."

"Yes, Mom, and we're a half mile away from you. Get your coat. We'll be there soon. We'll pick you up."

"I don't want to ride with Adrian. I'll take my own car. I'd rather—"

"No, Mom, you're too upset. You won't be any good to Drew if you're in an accident. Just stay there. We're a block away."

Karen felt a hand on her arm. She turned, and there he was again. Ari. His voice. *Go, Karen, now.* Then he was gone.

Karen didn't have the energy to fight. She looked out her window and saw the car lights in the driveway. Shaking, she gathered her coat and purse, locked the door, and walked outside. She almost tripped over Igor resting serenely on the sidewalk. Igor. He was always around when something important happened.

Jocelyn jumped out of the front seat of Adrian's car and opened the back door. "Hurry, Mom. Get in."

Karen glanced in the back and noticed Lisa on the other side.

"Oh, Mrs. Antilla, you can sit in the backseat with Jocelyn. I'll sit in the front." Lisa jumped out on her side the car.

"Good thinking," Jocelyn said. Lisa dashed around to the other side of the car and hopped in beside Adrian. Jocelyn climbed into the backseat on the driver's side next to her mother.

"Everyone ready?" Adrian asked in a soft husky voice.

When no one objected, the Audi sped off, and Karen turned to look out the rear window. Igor was gone.

CHAPTER 38

"Does anyone know anything?" asked Karen, her voice tight with desperation.

Jocelyn took her mother's hand. "We know Drew is unconscious and on the way to Hartford Hospital, Mom, if he's not there already. And we know he made at least two phone calls tonight, one to your answering machine and one to mine."

Karen looked confused. "But you were home, weren't you?"

"Yes, Mom, I was. I didn't answer the phone. I got the message right away though, tried to call him back, but the line was busy."

"How did he sound when he called you?"

"Disoriented. Something was wrong. He didn't finish speaking, and there was a crash. I think he dropped the phone."

Karen began to cry loudly. "He told me to go home, something was wrong. I should have known!" She pulled her hand away from Jocelyn.

"Who, Mom? Drew?"

Karen covered her face with both hands and wailed, "Oh, my poor baby! No one there for him when he needed help! I wasn't home!" Her shoulders heaved as she sobbed.

Jocelyn still didn't know who "he" was, but she let it go. Instead, she wrapped her arm around her mother's shoulders. "Mom, you can't blame yourself." Tears rolled down her own cheeks. "We just have to pray that Drew will be okay."

"I can't lose anyone else in my life," Karen whimpered.

"No, Mom, you won't." Jocelyn sounded a lot more confident than she felt. She knew she had to be the supporting beam for the family now. No one else was left to assume the role.

*   *   *

At ten-thirty, Adrian's Audi pulled into the hospital entrance. He drove directly to the emergency door.

"Jocelyn, you and your mother go in. Lisa and I will park the car and find you later."

Jocelyn and Karen hurried through the large automatic sliding doors. Once inside, Jocelyn spotted the information desk.

A uniformed woman looked up as they approached. "May I help you?" she asked before they could speak.

"Yes, we're the family of Drew Antilla," said Karen. "Has he been brought in?"

The receptionist checked her records. "Yes, he's here. Let me see what I can find out." She picked up the phone on her desk and pushed a number.

"This is Mary at the information desk. What is the status of Drew Antilla? His family is here. Dr. Callerman? Right. I'll tell them." She replaced the receiver.

"Dr. Callerman will be out in a few minutes to speak to you. He'll be able to tell you what's going on. Just have a seat please."

*   *   *

"Mrs. Antilla, I'm Dr. Callerman, the doctor in charge of the emergency room. I've been working with Drew since he was brought in by the paramedics an hour ago."

"How is he, Doctor?" Karen asked.

"He's in serious condition. When he arrived, he was unconscious, and he's still unconscious. It appears to be alcohol poisoning compounded by a possible Tylenol overdose. The paramedics brought along an empty Tylenol bottle that they found on a table near him."

Karen's hands flew to her face. "Oh, no, my baby! He'll come out of it, won't he? Please, God, let him come out of it!"

"We're doing the best we can, Mrs. Antilla. We won't know his prognosis for several hours."

Karen collapsed into sobs. Jocelyn stepped forward.

"Dr. Callerman, I'm Drew's sister. I'm the one who called 911. How were his vital signs when he was brought in?"

"His respiration and heart rate were both abnormally low as was his blood pressure, but he hasn't slipped further. We pumped his stomach. We have a tube inserted into his trachea to prevent choking and we're giving him oxygen and fluids by IV."

Karen stopped crying, but her face was the color of chalk. "Can we see him?"

"No, not at the moment. He's in Critical Care right now being monitored closely. We'll let you see him as soon as we can. Until then, a nurse or myself will keep you informed." Dr. Callerman glanced at Adrian and Lisa who were standing nearby, then turned back to Karen. "Are these other family members?"

Jocelyn answered for her mother. "They're friends of the family. We all drove together."

"Well, have a seat. Make yourselves as comfortable as possible. There's a cafeteria down the hall. We should be able to give you a better idea on how he's doing in an hour or so."

"Thank you, Doctor," Karen's voice quavered.

Dr. Callerman disappeared through the double doors, and Karen broke down again. Jocelyn put an arm around her mother and led her to a chair.

"Let's sit down, Mom. We'll have a while to wait." Jocelyn sat next to her mother. Adrian and Lisa sat in nearby chairs.

"Why? Why would he do such a thing?" Karen asked through her tears. "Do you think he has an alcohol problem?"

"I don't know, Mom. I'm wondering about that myself. He never used to drink." Jocelyn hesitated, wondering whether she should mention what happened on his recent visit to New York. "I guess this is no time for secrets. He got wasted the weekend he visited me. I was stunned. He seemed embarrassed, so we didn't talk about it. I thought it was a one-time thing."

"But the doctor also said something about Tylenol and an overdose. Oh god, do you suppose he . . . ?"

"I don't think so, Mom. That doesn't sound like Drew. I think it was an accident. Adrian, Lisa, what do you think?"

Lisa spoke slowly. "I've never met Drew, so I don't really know. But I imagine when the tests come back, they'll know how much alcohol he consumed and how many Tylenol he took. That should give you a clue."

Adrian leaned forward. "I once did a feature on on-campus drinking, and I learned that alcohol poisoning is very common at colleges. There are many incidents every year across the country. Most of them are accidental."

Karen looked in Adrian's direction briefly then turned away. She began to rummage in her purse. "I know I have more tissues in here somewhere."

Lisa pulled a package of tissues from her own purse and reached across Jocelyn to hand them to Karen. "Here, Mrs. Antilla, take these."

"Oh, thank you, dear," she said absently.

Jocelyn's eyes widened, and she smiled slightly at Lisa.

Adrian stood. "I'm going to the cafeteria for coffee. Can I bring something back for anyone?"

"Yes, I'm thirsty," Jocelyn said. "I'd like a soda, and bring one back for Mom too, please. Lisa?"

"I'm just fine with the water fountain, but thank you."

CHAPTER 39

Karen stared at the red light of the exit sign on the emergency door. This was all too familiar, too much like the time when Ari . . .

They sit on chairs in the hall in the special section of the hospital. Family only. Doctors orders. Four chairs. One for Drew, one for Jocelyn, one for her. An empty chair for Ari's mother who is outside smoking a cigarette. Again.

They wait for a nurse who will take them in, one at a time, for only a minute or two.

The waits are long. No one speaks. Finally, the nurse appears. It's her turn.

She walks to his bedside. Oxygen. Tubes. IVs. Monitors. Machines. Nurses and doctors in masks. His eyes are closed. She touches his hand, and his eyes open a crack. Today there is no smile on his face. Only pain.

He nods at her, tries to speak. She leans in close to hear.

"Please," he says.

What does he want?

His eyes open wide. Pleads.

"Adrian. See Adrian. Please."

Yes, of course. She blinks back tears, tries to smile. Of course, she says, I'll arrange it. Don't you worry, darling, I'll arrange it.

"Now. Please."

Yes, darling, it will be done. She smiles again, turns, and walks out the door.

Drew and Jocelyn watch as she returns to the hall. She does not sit. She tells them she needs to talk to someone for Ari. Make an arrangement. Then she will go home, she tells them. Surprise on their faces. They stare, confused. She does not explain.

Cannot explain.

"Stay," she says. "You can phone me at home. Later."

She walks away without looking back.

CHAPTER 40

An hour later, Karen jumped when Dr. Callerman spoke. "I have some good news. Drew is still unconscious, but his respiration and heart rate have improved, and his body is responsive to touch."

"Oh, dear," said Karen. "When will he come out of it?"

"I think Drew will rouse soon, but we're not out of the woods yet. Blood tests indicated an alcohol level of .27 when he was brought in, which is very high but not usually fatal. The acetaminophen level was also quite high and probably contributed to the coma. Luckily, he was brought in early enough that we could administer an antidote. We're doing further blood tests to check liver and kidney function because high levels of Tylenol can be potentially damaging to those organs."

"Good, you think he'll rouse soon." Karen repeated the doctor's earlier words in a trancelike monotone.

"Yes." Dr. Callerman smiled faintly. "I can let you in to see him, you and your daughter, separately, for just minute or two."

Karen rallied from her stupor. "Yes, I'd like to go in." She turned to Jocelyn. "Do you mind? You can go after me."

"No problem, Mom. Go ahead."

Karen followed Dr. Callerman through the double doors.

CHAPTER 41

A bright light like the sun on water. A shadow ripples in the light. Flowing closer.

It's not your time, Drew. Go back.

That voice, the shadow, was that Dad?

Oh god where am I? My head hurts. I can't open my eyes. Voices. Whose voices? All gray. Where am I? Let me up. I can't move.

"Step closer, Mrs. Antilla. Touch him. Tell him who you are."

"Drew, this is your mother. I'm here."

Mom? What? Here's here? Oh, my head hurts.

"He's doing better. He's more comfortable. We've been able to take him off the respirator and remove the trach tube."

I don't know that voice. Who are they talking about? Why can't I see?

"Drew, can you hear me? Son, please squeeze my finger if you know I'm here."

I hear you, Mom. I hear you.

"He might be able to hear you, Mrs. Antilla. We're hopeful. That's why we brought you to see him, if only for a moment. Sometimes it helps."

Where am I? I want to scream. Why . . . ?

"He isn't moving, Doctor. Drew, know that I love you. I'm here for you, baby. Please try to move your finger just a little if you know I'm here."

My finger. Why can't I move my finger?

"Mrs. Antilla, we should go now. We're monitoring him constantly, and we should know more by morning."

"Drew, I'll be back. As soon as I can. I'm waiting, with Jocelyn, right outside the door."

Can't open my eyes. Can't speak. Why can't I move? The darkness. Damn the darkness.

"Here's your brother, Jocelyn. Talk to him."

"Bro, it's me. I'm here. Mom's here. Doctor, he's not moving at all. He's so still."

"You can touch him, hold his hand," said Dr. Callerman.

Josey, I can hear you. I know you're here. You're touching me. I can feel it, but I can't tell you.

"Bro, if only you could open your eyes. Drew, let me know that you know I'm here. Give me a signal."

I'm trying, Josey. I'm trying.

"Jocelyn, we don't want to tire him out. Let's go now."

"Drew, I love you."

He could feel her hand on his face.

"I'll be back. As soon as the doctor says I can. Bye, bro."

Footsteps. Doctor. I'm somewhere with a doctor. My head hurts. My stomach. The dark tunnel. No more voices. Alone again.

Drew. You are meant to be of this earth. You have promise.

His voice again! Drew's eyes flew open, and he saw the room around him for the first time. A hospital. He was in a hospital. A man in green scrubs and a mask hovered over him.

"He opened his eyes," said the stranger. "Get Dr. Callerman."

CHAPTER 42

Karen sailed into the waiting room, a calm smile upon her face. Just being able to see her son had elevated her mood. When Jocelyn rose to take her turn with Drew, Karen seated herself in a chair opposite Adrian and Lisa.

She looked directly at Adrian. "Thank you," she murmured, her voice guarded but sincere.

"You're welcome, Karen."

"And Lisa," Karen continued, "thank you for coming. I hope we can meet again under more favorable circumstances. Which brings me to a thought I've had . . ." Karen's eyes moved from Lisa to Adrian and back. "There's no point in all of us sitting here all night. When Jocelyn comes back, the three of you can drive to my house. Jocelyn can return with my car, and the two of you can go back to the city. We'll, of course, let you know what is happening with Drew. But it does look like it's going to be a long haul here, and while I appreciate your support, I know you both have lives and jobs. Jocelyn and I can manage."

"Of course," said Adrian.

"Yes," murmured Lisa. "If we can be of assistance later, just say the word."

The double doors swung open once again to reveal Jocelyn. Karen presented her plan, and Jocelyn agreed. The trio departed quickly, leaving Karen alone in her corner of the waiting room.

But not for long. Slowly the chair Adrian had vacated suffused with the hazy and faintly bluish image of Ari. He smiled at her.

He's going to make it, Karen. Our boy's going to make it.

Again, Karen marveled that the voice seemed to be coming not from the image across from her, but from inside her own head.

"Why are you here?" she asked, hoping no one in the other areas of the waiting room could hear her.

He made an ironic smile. *Because you need me.*

Her eyes burned. "Well, whoever, or whatever you are, I just want Drew to recover so I hope you know what you're talking about."

Our boy needs help, Karen. There are many questions to be asked. Don't rule out anything.

The image in the chair turned from hazy to pale, to transparent, then disappeared altogether.

"Don't rule out anything," Karen said aloud, reflecting on the words. *What did that mean? Oh, god, was he trying to say it hadn't been an accident?* Her stomach elevator-dropped to the base of her spine, and her arms erupted in gooseflesh.

The double doors opened.

"Mrs. Antilla, good news! Drew is awake. Come quickly!"

Karen struggled to her feet and hurried after Dr. Callerman.

"Thank you, God," she murmured. *And you too, Ari*, she thought.

*   *   *

It was 5:00 AM when Jocelyn returned to the waiting room. To her surprise, her mother was smiling.

"Mom?"

"Your brother's awake, honey! They let me talk to him for a few minutes, and they think he's going to be okay!"

Jocelyn threw her arms around her mother and held her tight. "Thank God, Mom. Will they let me see him?"

"Probably by 7:00 AM or so. They're in the process of moving him to a regular room, and then we'll be at the whim of the floor nurses. Dr. Callerman will leave instructions that we can see him outside of regular visiting hours, but he's already stated we can't stay in the room for long periods."

"Did Drew tell you what happened?"

Karen shook her head. "No. I didn't ask. I just squeezed his hand and told him we loved him, that you were gone getting the car and would see him later. He squeezed my hand back and said he was glad we were all there, which was kind of odd, now that I think of it, since there was only me."

"Maybe he knew we were both in there earlier."

"Maybe he did," Karen agreed. "Sit down, honey, we've got to make a plan. As soon as it's a decent hour, I think we should call Grandma Antilla. She'll want to know about Drew, of course, and her place would be great for us to crash for a while. We're lucky she's in New Britain, only fifteen minutes away."

Jocelyn looked at her mother quizzically. "You haven't seen much of Grandma lately."

"Well, no, but she'll want to be here for Drew. I know that."

"Okay," said Jocelyn dubiously. "I need to call the restaurant as soon as someone's there and make arrangements too. And call Lisa and . . ." Her voice trailed off.

"Yes, dear, you should call Adrian as well." Karen's body stiffened as she gave her daughter a tight smile.

Jocelyn hugged her mother once more. "Bless you, Mom, you're trying. I can see that." She released Karen and stood back, brushing aside the tears that had escaped in spite her intense effort to keep them corralled. "Someday soon, Mom, but not today, we'll talk about this stuff."

Karen studied her daughter. "Yes, we will." She frowned for a moment. "But you're right, today we must concentrate on your brother and what has led him to this place. Dr. Callerman said because of the circumstances, Drew will be held over for psychiatric observation. And there are still some liver and kidney function test results to come back too. Later today, I think you and I should try to get hold of Colin to see what he might know. I did try to call their apartment while you were gone, but no answer."

"That's right, I forgot about Colin. Yes, definitely. I'd like to hear his take on things."

"Oh, and I can't forget to call Mr. McKinley." Karen made a face as she gathered her purse and coat and stood up. "Let's wander over to Drew's floor and see if they'll sneak you in for a moment or two."

Arm and arm, mother and daughter walked down the hall.

CHAPTER 43

From his hospital bed, Drew stared out the window of his room. Sitting up, he felt empty and light-headed. A flock of honking geese flapped across his view of the cloudless sky. *Still migrating, even in May,* he thought.

A gravelly voice brought his attention back to the room. Standing in the doorway was a tall bespectacled man with thinning gray hair, bushy eyebrows, and patchy beard that looked like it belonged on a cartoon character. He wore a red and purple Hawaiian shirt.

"Hello, Drew, I'm Dr. Manley, psychiatrist on staff," he said with a squinty-eyed smile. "Dr. Callerman has asked me to talk to you. Do you feel well enough?"

A wave of nausea passed through Drew's body, and his stomach churned. "Kind of weak yet. A psychiatrist? I don't need a psychiatrist." *Especially one in a red and blue aloha shirt,* he thought to himself.

The chair made a scraping sound as Dr. Manley pulled it closer to the bed. "Situations like yours, I'm always called in. Hospital policy." Dr. Manley reached into his flowered shirt pocket and pulled out a small leather notebook and a pencil. "How often do you use alcohol?"

Drew sank back and took a breath of the antiseptic air. His pillows felt hot. "Well, it was Saturday night. I had whisky, must have drunk too much."

The doctor cleared his throat. "You not only had too much whisky, you also took Tylenol. They said you drank beer too. My question again, how often do you use alcohol?"

The words echoed in the room. Drew shrugged. "Occasionally. Not often."

"Be specific." The squinty-eyed smile reappeared.

Drew closed his eyes. "I don't know. Not every day. Weekends mostly."

Dr. Manley scratched something in his notebook. "Okay, I'll accept that for now. Let's talk about something else. What's been happening in your life lately to make it difficult?"

Drew turned away from the doctor's gaze. He pulled one of his pillows out from behind and punched at it, trying to even it out. "I didn't say my life was difficult." He replaced the pillow.

"Oh, I know that, but let's just assume it is. What comes to mind?" The doctor tapped his pencil against his notebook.

Drew fingered the scratchy surface of the hospital coverlet. "Just flunked a big test, a test in my major. I'll probably fail the class."

The psychiatrist nodded and continued. "What else?"

Drew ran his tongue his lower lip and noticed it was sore. He must have bitten it earlier. "I met a girl at a party. She wanted to go out with me, but my roommate asked her out. He was at her house Saturday night. I blew my chance. As usual."

"Had you gone out with her, Drew?"

Why the hell did he have to ask so many questions? It was none of his business. "No, but I'd thought about asking her out." Drew knew he sounded irritated. "She'd been calling me."

Dr. Manley wrote again in his notebook. "I see. Anything else? How about your family? Parents? Siblings?" His voice fired like a shotgun.

"I have a mom and a sister. My dad died."

"How long ago did your dad die?"

"Two years . . . he had cancer."

"Sorry, Drew. I'm sure that was very hard." The psychiatrist leaned closer. His steely-gray eyes narrowed to slits. "Do you think about your dad often?"

Drew shifted sideways, away from the doctor. "Sure."

Dr. Manley tapped his pencil again. "Anything else about your family that would help me to know you better?"

Drew felt his face redden. "We found out . . . well, Dad told Mom he was gay."

"Your voice tells me this was hard for you, that it still is."

Drew stared at a crack in the ceiling on the other side of the room. "Sometimes I've thought . . ."

Dr. Manley remained silent.

Drew took a deep breath. "I'm useless, and I shouldn't . . ."

"Shouldn't what, Drew?"

"Shouldn't . . ." Drew grimaced. "Shouldn't have been born."

Dr. Manley leaned even closer, so close Drew thought he could smell the doctor's mouthwash. "Have you told anyone else your thoughts?"

Drew whispered, "Josey knows."

"Sorry, I couldn't hear you. What did you say?"

Drew spoke a little louder, focusing on the ceiling crack again. "Jocelyn, my sister Jocelyn, knows."

Dr. Manley kept writing. "Do you have plans for the future, Drew?"

Drew felt a weight lift. The subject had changed. "I'm majoring in business, like my dad."

"Was this your choice, or a choice someone made for you?"

"It was my choice." Drew glared at Dr. Manley.

The psychiatrist scribbled another note, then sat back in his chair, and removed his glasses. "I can see you're getting tired. There are just a few more questions I have to ask."

Drew shrugged. "Whatever."

"How much do you want to live, Drew?"

Drew stared at the floor. "I don't know. I haven't thought about it."

The psychiatrist looked at Drew squarely. "Did you plan to take your life?"

Drew met Dr. Manley's gaze. "What do you mean?"

"With alcohol and pills?"

"I wasn't planning anything."

"Your mother said you telephoned her. Your sister too."

"Did I?" Drew bit his lip again, this time noticing a salty taste.

"Were you calling for help, Drew?" The psychiatrist rifled through the pages of his notebook like a dealer shuffling cards.

"I don't know what you're asking, Doctor."

"Are you afraid you're gay like your father?"

Drew's face flamed. "No. What I'm afraid of is I'm a mistake!"

Dr. Manley put his glasses on again and smiled his waxen smile. "I don't have any more questions right now. I'm going to recommend that you stay in the hospital for several days. It's safe here, and I think you could use the time to work some things out. There are groups, you know, people to talk to. I'll be speaking with you again too. Every day."

"Yes, sir," said Drew, pulling up the covers. He could hardly wait.

CHAPTER 44

At 8:00 AM Sunday morning, Karen rang the doorbell of her mother-in-law's home. The chimes seemed to echo. She was more than a little nervous about how she would be received. After all, she'd only seen Helen once since the funeral, and that meeting had been disastrous.

"Do you suppose she's out?" asked Jocelyn, standing behind her mother. "I wouldn't think so."

The door flew open to reveal Helen in an elegant lavender taffeta bathrobe and matching high-heeled slippers. Helen's mouth dropped open for a moment at the sight of Karen, but quickly turned to a smile when she spied Jocelyn.

"Granbo," Jocelyn squealed, rushing past her mother to hug her grandmother.

"Sweetheart!"

There was no mistaking the affinity between them. Helen had always bonded strongly with children, a quality Karen had long envied. When it came to people, Helen was a pied piper, drawing everyone close to her.

Karen cleared her throat. "Good morning, Helen. Sorry to arrive unannounced."

"Oh, Good Lord, where are my manners?" Helen hugged Karen stiffly. "Come in, both of you. It's been so long. Let me make more coffee. I've emptied the pot already, been up since seven."

"Coffee would be good about now," Karen murmured as she looked around Helen's small but elegantly decorated home. Helen loved to surround herself with beautiful things. She always found a way to buy paintings, sculptures, and unique ornaments though her budget was modest.

"It's good to see you both," Helen shot over her shoulder. She patted her blonde hair into place as she swished down the hall to the kitchen, Jocelyn and Karen following. "But where's Drew? Haven't seen that boy in months, not even to get his haircut. No, wait, don't tell me. He's probably got a girlfriend keeping him busy. Right?"

Karen wondered how Helen could talk nonstop, especially since she was an incessant cigarette smoker. She never smoked in her house, only outside on the deck off the kitchen, not wanting to pollute her art objects.

Karen stood next to the counter, absently running a hand over the marble surface. "We've just come from Hartford Hospital, Helen. Drew was taken there by ambulance last night. Unconscious."

"No!" Helen's hands flew to her mouth, and her eyes widened. "Is he . . . ?"

"It looks like he's going to be okay. He's conscious now and speaking, but they need to continue monitoring him. They're running more tests."

"What happened?" Helen's robe rustled as she pulled it tighter around herself.

"Well, he . . . it was . . ." Karen swallowed. She hadn't had to tell anyone yet what had happened.

"Yes, Karen, go on," Helen implored.

"It was alcohol poisoning. He overdosed on liquor." She took a deep breath then let it out. "And there's more. He took pills too."

Helen wailed, "No, not Drew! I can't believe it, not after Nikko . . . or Annika!"

This time it was Karen's jaw that dropped as she grasped the connection. Grandpa Nikko! And Annika, Ari's sister! Both of them irrevocable alcoholics. Nikko, dead for ten years from cirrhosis of the liver. And Annika, somewhere in California, out of touch more than five years. Annika, who didn't even know Ari was dead.

"I don't think it's alcoholism," Karen stammered. "But clearly, he drank too much, too fast."

Her face pale from the news, Helen's lowered herself to a kitchen chair. Karen and Jocelyn followed suit. Forgotten was Helen's offer of coffee.

Jocelyn broke the silence. "He's been depressed since Dad died. It's been worse lately."

Karen's eyebrows raised slightly. "You knew that, Jocelyn? Why didn't I?"

Jocelyn shrugged. "I don't know, Mom. It was obvious to me."

Karen closed her eyes and leaned forward, one elbow on the table, supporting her head with her hand. "God, forgive me," she choked out. Tears flowed down her cheeks despite her closed eyelids.

A silence followed, finally broken by a warm hand on her arm. She opened her eyes. Jocelyn had reached out to her.

"It's okay, Mom," said Jocelyn softly. "Don't be too hard on yourself."

Too hard on herself. A familiar refrain. That's what Melissa had said, what, twelve hours ago? And to think she'd thought Jocelyn was the problem in the family then. Karen shook her head, amazed at how quickly life can change.

"I agree," Helen said, although her voice lacked conviction. "I think what you both could use right now is some sleep. The beds upstairs are made up with fresh sheets, lots of clean towels in the bathroom."

"I am exhausted," admitted Karen. "I don't know if I can sleep, but I think I should try."

The chair scraped as she rose to her feet. Her legs felt wobbly. "Coming, Jocelyn?"

Jocelyn, who appeared to be lost in thought, startled at the sound of her name. "Sure, Mom, but first I want to visit with Granbo a bit. I also want to see if I can catch someone at the restaurant. I need to let them know I won't be in tonight."

"As you wish, dear," said Karen. "I'll have to get hold of McKinley later, too, but right now, I'm going to try to rest. Thanks, Helen."

"No problem," Helen murmured. "Rest well. I'm glad it's Sunday, and I have no appointments in the salon. When do you think I can see Drew?"

Karen thought a moment. "This afternoon probably. He'll appreciate seeing you, I'm sure." She headed down the carpeted hall toward the stairs.

CHAPTER 45

Jocelyn waited until her mother was upstairs before turning to her grandmother. "Mind if I make a call, Granbo?"

"To work, you mean? Of course not."

"No, to someone else."

Her grandmother looked faintly surprised but shrugged her shoulders and said, "Of course, dear." She opened a drawer and pulled out a package of cigarettes. "I'm stepping out to the deck for a cigarette if you want to use the phone here in the kitchen."

"Thanks." She dialed Lisa's number. "Hi, Lisa. I'm at my grandmother's house. Great news, Drew came out of it, and they say he's going to be okay. No, I don't know when I'll be coming back. Mom needs me right now, and, of course, I want to talk to Drew. But I'll call when I know."

They chatted a while longer before Jocelyn began to feel guilty about her grandmother's phone bill.

"I should go, Lisa. Yes, I'm going to miss you too, especially after last night! We haven't had a chance to talk about that, but Lisa, wow! Gotta go now."

Jocelyn hung up the phone and turned around to see her grandmother standing in the kitchen doorway, smiling. She felt a rush of heat to her face. Her cheeks must be the color of Red Delicious apples.

"Ooh, la, la!" said Helen with a wink. "Sounds like my little granddaughter has herself a lover named Lisa."

"Oh, Granbo, I'm so embarrassed!"

"Don't be. Never be embarrassed by love."

Jocelyn grinned. "You've always been accepting." Granbo had met many different people through her shop. Although they'd never discussed it, Granbo had never shown any disapproval or even surprise at the news her son was gay.

"Granbo, did you know I was gay?"

Helen chuckled. "Yes, I had a feeling."

Jocelyn blushed again. "I think I've always known. But I didn't think anyone else could tell." She wondered if she should say more. *Sure, why not.* "Lisa is actually my first girlfriend."

"Really?" Helen's eyes widened. "Sit down, dear. Tell me about her."

They both took a seat at the kitchen table.

"I'm so in love. And scared."

"Scared? Why, dear?"

Jocelyn didn't know if she could put it into words. "Everything's happened so fast. We met, fell in love, got, you know . . ." Her cheeks felt hot again. "Intimate." *Oh boy, that was a mouthful.*

Helen seemed unruffled. "So, what's scary about that? You'll probably fall in love half a dozen times at least!"

"That's the thing. I want what I have with Lisa to last forever. But since I've never been in love before, I'm afraid it won't last. Does love ever work out?"

Helen laughed. "Not according to the soaps or my clients."

"Oh, Granbo, you and your soaps," Jocelyn giggled. Her grandmother had followed those soap operas for as long as she could remember. Jocelyn was sure that one of the reasons Granbo's clients were so faithful to her was the jovial tell-all atmosphere she encouraged in her home salon, built by Grandpa Nikko before his bad years.

"Seriously, dear, about love working out, why not?" Helen reached out to tuck a lock of hair behind Jocelyn's ear. "Probably the odds are against it, but who cares? Why pay any attention to statistics and glum forecasts? Make your own rules, I say. Love as hard as you can for as long as you can, and most important, have fun while you're at it. To hell with anyone who says anything different!"

Jocelyn could see the fire in her grandmother's eyes as she spoke. She remembered that when she was a little girl, Granbo said the worst crime in life was to be a bore, a crime Granbo herself certainly hadn't committed. Jocelyn had always thought she might be a bit like her grandmother. She hoped so anyway.

Sometimes she wished her mom was more like Granbo, but then she'd remember how organized Mom always was, and dependable, whereas

Granbo . . . well, you never knew what she'd do from one day to the next. Though she loved her Granbo dearly, she had to admit she was rather impulsive.

But on this traumatic day, Granbo was here for Jocelyn, Drew, and even for her mother.

*　　*　　*

Jocelyn and Helen walked down the hospital corridor, their heels clicking on the hard, polished linoleum floor. Helen carried a vase of lilacs. They stopped in front of the closed door of room 34.

"This is it," Jocelyn said to her grandmother as she opened the door.

"Hey, Drew. Look who I brought." Jocelyn pulled her grandmother into the room.

"Granbo!" Drew's face lit up for an instant. Helen set the flowers on the nightstand then wrapped her arms around him. He buried his face in her warm, comforting shoulder. "I'm so ashamed."

Helen separated from him to hold his face in her hands. Looking straight into his eyes, she said, "We love you, Drew, and that's all that matters. The rest we'll figure out later."

Drew leaned toward the flowers on the nightstand and inhaled their fragrance. "Lilacs from your yard, Granbo! I've always loved your lilacs."

"I remembered that," Helen said smoothly, taking a chair.

Drew looked around in confusion as Jocelyn and Helen took a seat. "Where's Mom?"

"Talking with some doctor," Jocelyn replied. "A Dr. Manfred or something."

"Dr. Manley," Drew corrected. "The Gestapo. I mean, my therapist." He grimaced.

"Ah, yes," said Helen, matching Drew's look. "The fearsome Dr. Manley. Tightlipped, no-nonsense type, I'm sure. Undoubtedly with all sorts of theories." Helen spat out the last word as though she had a bad taste in her mouth.

Drew guffawed. Probably for the first time in days, Jocelyn speculated. Granbo had that effect on people.

Helen's face became serious. "Well, listen up, young man. We're going to get you well, and there will be no buts about it. What's this about drinking? Don't you remember your grandpa and Aunt Annika? If you think that has nothing to do with you, you're wrong. That's in your blood, Drew. Not saying you have a problem, but you have to consider maybe you could get yourself into a drinking problem faster than other people." She shook her head. "Your grandpa Nikko. I saw it with him. Such a good man, but he always kept everything inside, you know."

She paused long enough to take a breath, but not long enough to give anyone else a chance to speak. "It's not healthy, Drew. I don't know all the fancy terms, but I know that. Years before anyone had any idea of what might have been on Grandpa's mind, he was drinking by himself in the basement. It killed him, Drew, and we still don't know what he was thinking. Drew, baby, don't do that to yourself. Promise me. Open your mouth and talk to these fancy-pants therapists or whatever they have around here."

Drew smiled weakly. "Okay, Granbo. I'll try."

Jocelyn chuckled. Helen never minced words. Jocelyn didn't either, but somehow, people didn't react to her the way they did to Granbo. People took offense to her words, but Granbo always came off as charming.

The door creaked open, and a striking young Asian woman with long dark hair walked in. She wore a short-sleeved white shirt and navy cargo pants. "Oh, excuse me. I didn't know anyone was here," she said. "I'll come back later."

"That's okay," said Jocelyn, noting the badge on the woman's shirt pocket. "Are you a nurse?"

"No, I'm one of the paramedics who brought Drew in last night. My name's Jade Tanaka. Just wanted to come by and see how he is." She grinned at Jocelyn then turned to Drew. "You're looking much better than the last time I saw you. Glad you're doing okay. I'll stop by later."

"No, stay. Please. We don't mind," said Jocelyn. "You saved Drew's life. We can't thank you enough."

Jade smiled at Jocelyn. "Thanks, but I'm part of a team." She turned to address Drew. "I'm the one who put the trach tube in. My partner started the IV."

Drew's face reddened and he pulled his sheets close around himself. "Thanks. I don't know what you saw. I mean, I don't know what to say."

Jade took his hand, squeezing it briefly. "It's okay, you don't have to say anything. I'm just glad to see you alert and sitting. Our cases don't always . . ." her voice trailed off. "Anyway, I'm on shift in a few, so I can't stay." She turned to leave.

"Wait," said Jocelyn. "Can I have a word with you? For just a sec? In the hall as you walk, maybe?" She ignored the astonished looks on the faces of her grandmother and Drew.

"Sure. Hope you can walk fast," Jade said laughing.
"You bet."

* * *

"So, what's up?" Jade asked once they were in the hall.

How could Jocelyn explain that she suddenly knew what she wanted to do with her life? All it took was seeing this woman in her medic uniform, thinking about her in the ambulance tending to Drew and *wham*, Jocelyn knew. This was it. Breathlessly she blurted out, "How do I become a paramedic?"

Jade studied her face. "So, you got the call, did you? Well, it's not hard if you're willing to work. What you do is apply to a hospital or a fire department that sponsors paramedic students, and if accepted, you take your training. Wait." She stopped in her tracks and dug a small notepad and a pen out of her shirt pocket. "Give me a call at this number, and I can explain more, if you're interested. Or call one of the training facilities."

Jocelyn took the piece of paper, folded it carefully, as if it were a thousand dollar bill. "I'll do that," she murmured staring at the name and phone number. When she looked up, Jade had already disappeared.

CHAPTER 46

The following afternoon, Drew fidgeted with the remote trying to decide if he should watch TV for a while. Probably some hospital person would appear any minute. Why couldn't he just leave this place? He felt better. Headache gone. Stomach back to normal. Not so dizzy anymore.

As he sped through the channels, he heard footsteps in the hall. The door opened. Colin edged into the room. God, how did he find out so fast?

"Man, what are you doing here?" Drew asked.

Colin positioned himself at the foot of Drew's bed. "Your mom called yesterday afternoon and told me what happened. She said I could visit today."

"So I got drunk. I feel kind of stupid lying here." Drew climbed out of bed and wrapped a hospital robe over his pajamas.

Like an anxious stork, Colin shifted his weight from one foot to the other.

Drew waved his arm at a chair near the window. "Sit down."

Colin continued to shift back and forth. "Uh, Drew, Grace is here too. She's waiting outside. She wanted to come along even though . . . Well, you know. I told her I'd ask you first. You mind?"

Drew slumped into a sitting position on the edge of the bed. *Oh, great.* Now Grace would see him looking like this too. Damn his mother, what the hell was she thinking, telling his business around campus, inviting people to see him? "What the hell. I don't care."

Colin stopped shuffling. "I'll get her then. But before that, I just want you to know I'm sorry."

Drew studied his hands. "About what?"

Colin's voice was even gruffer than usual. "Sorry I . . . I'm sorry about what happened."

"Forget it," Drew interrupted. "Go get Grace." He didn't want to talk about any of this. When Grace entered the room, Drew started to rise, but Grace insisted he stay put. "How are you doing, Drew?" she asked, a look of concern in her eyes.

Drew sank back on the bed. "Fine, hanging in there. Grab a chair. Good view of the parking lot from here." He forced a smile, as he motioned them to the seats next to the window.

Once seated, Colin cleared his throat. "I don't know what to say. I didn't know."

"Nothing to say. I kind of lost it, I guess." *God this felt awkward.* Drew fingered the remote control.

Grace blurted, "Hey, *lost it* is an understatement. Colin told me what happened. Are you going to be okay?"

Drew leaned back, supporting himself with his arms. "By the time the doctor and the shrink finish with me, who knows?"

Colin looked surprised. "Shrink? What for, man?"

Drew was pissed. He didn't feel like reciting a grocery list of all the ugly details. "Do I have to draw you a picture?" he snapped.

"Hey, don't be so touchy. I didn't know you were going to drink all that booze."

Drew hoped a nurse or someone would walk into the room. Grace and Colin were the last people he wanted to talk with about this. "Don't worry about it. I fucked up. What's new with you?"

Grace blinked several times as though she was trying not to burst into tears. "There've been a lot of changes for me lately." She exchanged a glance with Colin then turned back to Drew.

Drew looked out over the parking lot to avoid her soft brown eyes. He dropped his voice and said, "Thanks for coming." He didn't know what to say. She hadn't cared about him those nights she was fucking Colin.

"How long are you going to be here, man?" Colin asked, obviously trying to change the subject.

"Not sure yet."

"Any good looking nurses?"

"Hey, nurses are nurses. Give me a break." Drew picked up the remote again.

Grace jumped in. "Are you going back to school to finish the semester?"

Hell, how did he know? "Don't think so. I really fucked up the math exam. Colin must have told you that. I'm a lost cause. A loser. No sense going back."

"I'm sorry, Drew," said Grace.

Damn, he didn't want to be pitied.

"It'll be empty at the apartment without your ass there," said Colin.

Sure, Colin would think about the apartment. He really didn't know where he'd go when he left the hospital, but he wouldn't go back to school. "You won't notice. We hardly talked anyway. Just turn on the TV and pretend I'm there." Drew attempted a smile.

Colin grinned. "I don't even know if I can work the remote control."

Grace spoke up. "Hey, Colin, could I talk to Drew a few minutes alone?"

"Yeah, sure. I just remembered something. Need to go back to the car." Colin looked almost eager to go. "Back in a few."

Grace pulled her chair a little closer to the bed. She reached over and touched Drew's arm. "I heard you almost died."

Her hand rested on his arm like a heavy weight. "Well, *almost* isn't dead." He moved his arm, pretending he needed to scratch his nose.

"I'm sorry about that time you walked in on us in your apartment."

Drew looked at the floor. "I was pretty stupid to open the door."

"Did you know that you were the one I wanted to date? I went out with Colin because you didn't ask. It's probably not the best time to be telling you this."

Drew's laugh was bitter. "Story of my life. Just friends. I'm used to that." Used to that? Heck, he didn't have any friends.

Grace continued, "You know the night of that party when we met? I drank way too much. Made an ass of myself."

"You were okay," he said in a monotone. *Why bother talking about it now?*

Grace spoke softly. "I got a ticket for a DUI two weeks ago. My dad blew up."

"Well, I never drank and drove."

"That's one of your 'not yets' then."

"One of my what?" Drew asked.

"Your 'not yets.' The things that haven't happened to you yet but will if you keep drinking. It's only a matter of time, Drew. I didn't think I had too much to drink. It was after I took Colin home one night."

"Why are you telling me this?"

"I just want you to know that I think, no, I know, that I have a drinking problem too."

Drew stared out the window again. He wished he could be one of the people walking to a car in the parking lot.

"I've been going to a program. And AA too." She paused and followed Drew's eyes out the window. "I haven't had a drink now in two weeks."

"You're kidding." Drew was stunned.

"Yeah, well most people wouldn't have figured. My parents didn't. It really sneaked up on me. The night I met you, and the time with Colin, and the DUI were just a few of my drinking incidents. But the DUI was the thing that forced me to see my drinking was out of control. I'm going to AA on campus. Just in case you ever think about going."

"So why did you want to talk to me without Colin in the room?"

"It's obvious, isn't it? I'm not proud of what happened."

"Not your fault." Why did she have to make him uncomfortable?

An awkward silence hung in the room.

Grace stood. "I'll get Colin, if that's okay. He's probably had enough fresh air."

Drew forced a smile. "I'm sure he's scoped out the nurses by now."

In a short time, Grace returned to Drew's room with Colin, who carried a white plastic grocery sack.

Colin said, "Hey, man, how's the food here?"

Same old Colin. Doesn't really have a clue. Like he wanted to eat after what he'd been through. But Colin was always hungry.

"I haven't eaten much. Haven't felt like eating. Maybe today." He continued to play with the remote, wishing his visitors would leave. Then he remembered. "Colin, what about the fish?" he asked in a panic. "Are you feeding your fish?"

"Oh, sure. They were all staring at me on Sunday, and it dawned on me you weren't around to feed them. I've remembered ever since."

"Thank God," said Drew in relief as he set the remote on his nightstand. "By the way, what's in the sack?"

"Oh. Almost forgot about that." Colin opened the sack and produced Drew's most recent sketchbook. "I thought this might help you pass the time. You used to like to draw stuff."

Grace looked as astonished as Drew felt at Colin's apparent consideration. "Thank you," said Drew, reaching out to accept the sketchbook. "I'm surprised you thought of that."

Colin shuffled uncomfortably. "Hey, man, I was cleaning up, and I saw it."

Just then there was a knock on the door, and Dr. Manley appeared, this time in a pink and green aloha shirt. "Hi, Drew. Time for our session."

Drew set the sketchbook next to the remote and the flowers on his nightstand, dreading the next pleasurable activity of the day.

CHAPTER 47

Dr. Manley studied Grace and Colin as they exited, closing the door behind themselves. "Is that the girl you met at the party? The one who went out with your roommate?"

Drew sighed. Dr. Manley didn't miss a trick. "Yes, it was. And the guy was Colin, my roommate."

"What's her name?" asked Dr. Manley, surreptitiously sliding his notebook and pencil out of his shirt pocket.

"Grace," said Drew in a flat voice as Dr. Manley scribbled a note to himself.

"So, tell me again how you met."

"At a party. She was drunk, and she clung to me like a piece of plastic wrap."

"Were you drunk too?"

"No, I never get drunk at parties." He picked up the pitcher of ice water from his moveable table and poured himself a glass.

"Do you go to many?"

"No." He took a swallow of water. "But when I do, I'm usually the driver."

"So, are you telling me you never get drunk?" Dr. Manley locked eyes with Drew.

Drew hesitated, but he couldn't look away. It would be ridiculous to lie. "No," he said.

"When was the last time? The time before last Saturday."

Drew ran his fingers through his hair. "Oh, in my apartment, I guess. The time before that, at my sister's when she was out. Usually in my apartment though but only beer."

"Alone?"

Drew blinked. He'd never thought about that. "I guess," he answered.

"More often than people know?"

Drew's face reddened. "Yeah, I suppose."

Dr. Manley scratched several more notes before looking up. He nodded toward the nightstand. "I see you have a notebook, too."

Drew glanced at it. "Oh yeah, that. It's a sketchbook."

"Yours?" asked the doctor.

Drew nodded.

"Mind if I look?"

"If you want."

Dr. Manley leafed through the sketchbook, stopping at several drawings. "Lovely fish, Drew. Isn't this a betta?"

"Yes. All the fish belong to Colin, but I used to feed them."

"And this last one, the deer. Outstanding."

"Oh, that one's not finished. I'd forgotten about it. Haven't touched that book in months."

"Well, it looks finished to me. You've captured this doe perfectly, in a frozen moment of fear. Do you ever feel like that?"

Drew considered for a moment. "No. Well, maybe, but this drawing doesn't remind me of myself, it makes me think of my mother."

"Uh, huh," said Dr. Manley, placing the sketchbook back on the nightstand in order to scratch more notes. "Let's talk about your father."

In the middle of another sip of water, Drew almost choked. As soon as he'd mentioned his mother, he anticipated Dr. Manley would start asking questions about her. But no, this bizarre psychiatrist starts asking about his father. Unbelievable.

"What about him?" Drew asked. "You already know he was gay."

"True," said Dr. Manley, "but how did you feel about that when you found out?"

Drew shrugged. "Surprised, but an even bigger surprise had been that my dad was dying. Both pieces of news made me feel kind of . . . frozen, I guess."

"Like the deer?"

Drew stared at Dr. Manley then answered evenly, without emotion. "Yes, I suppose."

"Are you afraid you're gay, Drew?"

A jolt of anger rushed through his body. Drew was furious. "No, damn it! You already asked, and I told you. I'm not gay, and I'm not worried about being gay. I have never had an erection thinking about a man!"

Dr. Manley grinned. "So, I'm gathering you've had one or two thinking about a woman?"

Drew folded his arms across his chest and gave Dr. Manley a disgusted look.

"Okay, okay." Dr. Manley placed his notebook and pencil into his shirt pocket then turned his attention back to Drew. "Let's move on. Did your father have many lovers?"

"No, just one. That's what he told us anyway."

Dr. Manley stood and began to pace with his hands in his trouser pockets. "Did he have this lover when he died?"

"Yes."

"Have you ever met him?"

"No. Well, sort of. At the hospital when Dad died. At the funeral. And Josey tells me he drove her and Mom to this hospital on Saturday night when I was admitted."

"Really," said Dr. Manley, raising his eyebrows.

"Yes," Drew volunteered. "It was news to me, but he and Josey see each other all the time. Mom didn't know either."

"So how do you feel about that?" Dr. Manley asked as he jingled the change in his trouser pockets.

This time, Drew grinned. "Like the doe," he answered.

Dr. Manley chuckled. "I think that's how I would feel too, Drew, under the circumstances." He took his hands out of his pockets and studied his watch.

"One more thing, Drew, and we'll wrap it up for today. Do you think you have a drinking problem?"

Drew shrugged. "I don't know. Most people I know drink. Colin drinks, but I don't think he has a problem. Grace drinks too, but she told me just now that she's quit and is going to AA. She's a social drinker though, and I was not."

"Uh huh," said Dr. Manley, rubbing his goatee, "but there are many kinds of drinkers. To be honest, I think you may have a problem, since you drink alone to the point of intoxication. But we'll talk about that more on another day."

He nodded his head toward Drew's sketchbook. "Why don't you do some more drawing while you're here?"

Without waiting for an answer, Dr. Manley patted Drew on the arm and strode toward the door. "See you tomorrow," he said over his flowered shoulder.

CHAPTER 48

Having missed a meeting, Karen was more anxious than usual to meet with her Thursday group. Everyone seemed to detect her need to talk the moment she walked through the door. Dismissing the usual introductions, Roberta encouraged Karen to tell her story.

"It's entirely my fault," said Karen, after telling them that Drew had been in the hospital. Her eyes glazed with tears. "If I'd been more aware of what my son was thinking, I could have helped him. The last several days have been hard." She dapped at her eyes with a Kleenex.

"We're here to listen," said Baxter, pushing up his glasses.

The group paid rapt attention as Karen recounted the events of the past twelve days.

" . . . And that's most of it. Jocelyn and I are both back at work. Drew has been released from the hospital and is staying with Ari's mother, going through outpatient treatment and to AA for a while."

"Ari's mother? That's a surprise. I thought you didn't get along," Roberta said.

She winced. "We don't. Not since Ari died. I did something that angered her, and she hasn't forgotten." It was still painful for her to think about.

"How did you get on her wrong side?" Tom asked. Of course, the master of bluntness would ask that question.

Karen's shoulders tightened. "It's a long story. I don't want to go into it right now."

"I could write a book about being on the outs with people," groaned Lucille. "That's life as I know it."

"How long is Drew staying with his grandmother?" Baxter changed the subject.

"At least a month. His psychiatrist thought he should continue there rather than looking for a program here."

Roberta looked directly at Karen. "You can't redo the past. You can only go forward. Drew is working with some good people. But here and now, our concern is you."

Lucille twisted a strand of hair around her little finger. "I don't know. This relates to me too. I'm worried about what will happen to my three children if their father leaves. It's hard enough growing up without bringing more problems into their lives."

Tom smirked. "Everything always relates to you."

Karen spoke again, ignoring Tom and Lucille. "What's most important is my children are both alive. Nothing else matters now. Jocelyn being gay . . ." She rolled her eyes. "Oh well."

"Sounds like you've had quite a wake-up call," said Roberta.

*   *   *

Karen and Melissa walked together to the parking lot. "Exhausting session, tonight," said Karen. "I can't remember when I've felt this drained."

"Too tired for coffee?" asked Melissa.

"Maybe another time," Karen apologized.

"What about Sunday afternoon? I was thinking about taking a bike ride. Would you be interested?"

"Well, I haven't ridden . . . But Jocelyn's bike is still in the garage." She frowned for a moment then turned to Melissa with a smile. "Yes! I think a bike ride would be good." She pictured the garage door opening. An automatic door.

CHAPTER 49

*A*n automatic door swings open. She steps outside. She is crying so hard she can barely see ahead. The car, where's the car? Suddenly, a voice—it's Helen. Outside smoking.

"Where are you going," Helen wants to know.

Home, she says.

"No! You can't! Can't leave him now! So little time!"

Can't stay. Can't talk. Sorry, she says.

"How can you!"

A hand on her arm, pulling. Jocelyn. Must have followed her out.

"Mom, come back!"

Jocelyn, pulling, crying, pleading. Helen angry. Adrian, on the way. Ari dying. Wanting Adrian, not her. Ari, oh, Ari. She feels the clenched fist in her gut.

I'm sorry, she whispers, but I can't. Just can't.

"Karen, if you leave now, I'll never forgive you."

Helen's voice, so hard, so cold. So angry. Jocelyn, sobbing hard.

"Please, Mom!"

She finds the keys in her pocket, opens the door, gets in.

"How can you do this? You're a deserter," Helen screams. "How can you not say good-bye!"

She starts the motor, finds reverse. Backs up, then sees Helen and Jocelyn in the rearview mirror. Doesn't anyone understand, she asks the empty car. How could she possibly say good-bye with him there? Oh, Ari. How can you humiliate me like this?

CHAPTER 50

It had been a grueling day at school. Karen was so glad to be home to her dinner of leftover pork chops and her faded blue recliner. At last she could sit with her feet up, shoes kicked off.

Spring was in the air. Even her good classes were wild. Students blurting out, forgotten assignments, interruptive announcements over the loudspeaker.

But at least Roger Delacroix was doing better in math, thanks to her tutoring. He might even get a B this quarter. Helping him after school had been worth it, and since the individual help had started, he hadn't pulled any shenanigans in class either.

Maybe she'd watch some TV. She hadn't watched television in weeks, since before Drew's emergency. *Darn, where was that remote?* She chuckled to herself as she thought about the remote, which had always been Drew's toy. Since he'd been five years old, he'd been the keeper of the remote.

Her thoughts were interrupted by the ring of the telephone. Who'd be calling her tonight? She'd talked to both Drew and Jocelyn last night. Maybe it was Melissa.

"Hello," Karen answered cheerfully.

"Hello, Karen?"

A man's voice resonated. It sounded vaguely familiar to her, but she couldn't put a name with it. Times like this, she wished she had caller ID.

"Yes, this is Karen."

"Karen, this is Adrian."

Then a pause.

Karen felt the blood rush out of her face. "Oh, Adrian. I really can't—"

"How's Drew doing?"

She took a deep breath. "Well . . . Drew is doing as well as can be expected."

"I'm glad to hear that. I haven't talked to Jocelyn in several days. I've tried to get hold of her to ask about her brother, but she must be pretty busy with work."

Spending lots of time with Lisa too, Karen was sure. But Adrian didn't say that. "Well, I caught her at home yesterday late in the afternoon before she went to work. So she's around." Why did she feel the need to talk about her daughter's whereabouts with this man anyway? She still didn't like the idea of Jocelyn spending time with Adrian, but she'd keep that thought to herself.

"Is he responding well to the therapy?"

"Yes, he seems to be. He spends a lot of time with an outpatient group. He relates well to the young facilitator."

"I'm glad to hear that, Karen. When I was a young man, a few years older than Drew, I was part of a group too. It helped to have others to talk with. I'm sure he will benefit from having support in his life right now."

Karen bristled. How dare he imply that she hadn't been supportive of Drew. And she didn't care to hear about Adrian's younger years either. He didn't need to rub salt in her wounds. "Yes," she said, hearing herself speak in a clipped voice. "He's doing fine."

"I didn't mean to suggest you weren't supportive of Drew. I'm sure you were. But it's hard for a parent to know everything that's going on in a young person's mind. If nothing else, it's a generational thing."

Hell, what did he know about parenting? He was never married. Never had kids. "I understand," she said aloud. "Anyway, thanks for your concern. And, oh, thanks for your help that night. For insisting Jocelyn call 911. For bringing Jocelyn, me, and—"

"Don't mention it. My other reason for phoning is I have something that belongs to you." He spoke quickly, his words running together. "It's from Ari. A gift."

Karen's stomach churned. "From Ari? I don't understand."

"I can't explain on the phone, Karen. I've had it a while, but the timing hasn't been right until now. I'd like to find a convenient time to deliver it to your house."

What could this be? A trick of some kind? Ari had been dead more than two years. "I'll let you know, Adrian. You've caught me off guard."

"I understand."

"I'll let you know. Thanks for calling."

"Thanks for talking. I'm glad Drew is doing better. I was worried about him. If there's anything I can do to help in any way, just ask. Good-bye, now."

Karen hung up the phone. *A gift. Ari had never mentioned a gift. What now?*

CHAPTER 51

Karen and Melissa wound their way along the off-road bike path of the parkway.

"I haven't been on a bike in five years," Melissa said, pedaling her new Trek Hybrid bike that the young man in the bike shop had convinced her was the way to go. "This really feels good."

Melissa wore biking shorts and a tie-dyed T-shirt and windbreaker. "I bought this bike and these biking shorts yesterday. I figure even though I plan to lose weight, I have to accept the weight I am right now and buy clothes to fit rather than not buying new clothes at all."

Karen glanced down at her outfit, a pair of Bermudas and a zippered sweatshirt with a New York City T-shirt underneath. "I've had to do that too, Melissa. If I continue to bike, I'll get some biking shorts too. They're probably more comfortable than these cotton shorts. Say, you think five years is a long time? Ari and I got rid of our bikes when the kids were both in grade school. I'm glad Jocelyn's Le Monde was still in the garage. This feels great."

The bike trail meandered through the woods, crossed over a small creek, and passed through meadowlands. Karen felt one with the bicycle, alive, intense, and invincible. She hadn't felt like this in a long time. The outdoor air and the sun overhead were as good for her mind as the ride itself was for her body.

"Karen, this parkway is absolutely beautiful. I'm so glad you suggested it. It's not very busy today, and we can ride side by side as we talk. Ideal."

"Ari and I rode this route a few times before we gave up our bikes. I'm glad you like it." Her muscles tightened, heart pounded, and the pedals whirled faster and faster. "How about Jack and you? Where did you go?"

"We used to take our bikes in the van to a rural area to ride. That way we got to see different sights away from the city. But I must say this is a beautiful path and so close, too. Easy for us to meet and bike, without either of us having to haul a bike in the car. I can see doing this more often."

"Oh, I'd like that. I hope Jocelyn doesn't decide to reclaim her bike." Karen laughed.

Melissa was beginning to breathe hard. "Slow down a bit, will you? I'm really out of shape. Tell me, how's Drew doing?"

Karen slowed. She didn't want Melissa to overdo it. "Okay, I think. I visited him yesterday at Helen's. He told me he doesn't mind going to group, and he likes Dr. Manley. Says he isn't too bad to talk to."

Melissa caught her breath. "Whew, I'm glad you slowed down a little. Damn, this weight is a bitch. How often does he talk to Dr. Manley?"

Karen couldn't believe how easily her enjoyment of biking came back. Why hadn't she biked all along? She felt invigorated. "Right now it's every other day. I think it will lessen if Dr. Manley sees that he's doing well in the group setting."

"Slow down some more! This is a steep hill. Not used to hills," Melissa gasped. "Glad he's doing well. Frightening for you."

Karen slowed the pace. Even though Melissa had suggested biking, she felt she was the one in charge. "It's amazing how something like this can happen without anyone expecting it," Karen said.

"Tell me about it, Karen. I think we've both experienced things we didn't expect."

That was an understatement. "No kidding. Neither of us saw the clues. Say, do you ever hear from Jack?"

"Oh, he's living with someone now. I don't know how seriously he's involved, but at least it sounds as if he's not hanging around the bars. I hope he's telling whoever he's fucking about being HIV positive. I doubt it though. Usually just thinks of himself."

They reached the top of the hill and were on level ground again. Karen picked up the pace. "I hope your luck holds, Melissa. Not testing HIV positive, I mean. I remember the long week's wait after my own AIDS test."

"So far, so good. The longer I go without problems, the less angry I am. Give me another year and maybe I'll be close to normal again."

"I wonder when I'll be close to normal. I still have a hard time forgiving Ari for what he did to all of us. I still wonder if I'd been a better wife, if I'd have done things differently, if that would've helped. It's good to be able to admit it to someone instead of keeping everything inside."

"I know what you mean. Those questions always surface." Melissa wiped her face with the sleeve of her Windbreaker then stopped to take it off. "Whew, I need to recuperate from that hill. I hope there aren't any more like that." She climbed back on her bike. "On another note, how's Jocelyn?"

"Ah, I have some good news there. She's put in applications to paramedic schools, and I just heard yesterday she was accepted by a hospital. In fact, it's the same hospital where her girlfriend works as a physical therapist."

Melissa fumbled with the gears. "I'm trying to give myself an easier ride. I have to figure out these gears all over again. That's good news about Jocelyn. But do you think working at the same hospital as the girlfriend is a good idea? I mean, how committed are they?"

"We don't talk about that much. It's still not easy for me to talk about. For her either. But I accept that it's her life. She's an adult, and Lisa is a nice enough person. I don't know if working in the same hospital is a good idea or not. Time will tell, I guess."

"We seem to be winding our way out of the parkway. I see the city streets ahead. Hey, Karen, are you interested in stopping for an ice cream or a soda? Looks like there's a drive-in ahead."

Karen's legs were beginning to feel like rubber, despite her enjoyment of the ride. "Looks like the drive-in has picnic tables outside too. We can just pull up with our bikes. I definitely could use a rest." She thought she saw a look of relief on Melissa's face.

* * *

"This ice cream cone is just what I need," said Karen.

"Me too. Double turtle sundae hits the spot. I talk about cutting back, but never manage to do it."

"Now you're the one beating yourself up, Melissa."

"Well my weight is just another thing I blame on Jack. When I gained weight, I figured that's why he wasn't interested in sex any more. It was easier to blame the weight gain than to see what was really going on. But look at me. Jack's gone, and I'm still fat."

"It will happen, Melissa. I have to do something about my weight too. Biking today was a good start. For both of us. Perhaps we could join a gym."

Melissa smiled widely. "Good idea. If I put my money where my mouth is, that could help. And if we did it together, it would keep me honest!"

"Oh, yes," Karen laughed. "Important to keep ourselves honest!"

Melissa hesitated, as if trying to decide whether to speak or not. She cleared her throat. "Speaking about being honest, I'm wondering if you'd tell me what Ari's mother has never forgiven you for. You mentioned it Thursday night. Would it help to talk?"

Karen's smile disappeared. She bit her lip and began, her voice soft and low. "It happened at the hospital when Ari was there for the last time."

Melissa nodded but said nothing. She put her hand on her friend's arm.

Tears welled in Karen's eyes. "Only immediate family was allowed in his room to see him. He faded in and out of consciousness. Me. Drew. Jocelyn. His mother. Ari begged me to let him see Adrian, implored me to give the hospital permission for him to visit. Ari knew it wouldn't be too long. We all knew."

"What did you say?"

Karen continued. Melissa's presence was a blur. "I was so hurt, so angry. How could he ask that?"

"But what did you say?"

"I said I'd take care of it." Karen paused, wiped her eyes with the napkin. "I arranged with the nurses for him to see Ari. And then I left the hospital. Helen was outside. I told her I was going home. I never returned. He died a few hours later."

Melissa handed Karen an extra napkin. "Oh, Karen, I'm so sorry."

"Ari's mother never forgave me for not coming back."

"Karen, I don't know if I should ask or not, but I will. Maybe it would help to talk about it. Do you regret not having gone back to see Ari again?"

Tears ran down Karen's face. She hadn't realized how close to the surface tears still were. She swabbed at them with her very wet napkin. "You know, I think I've said all I can say about it today."

"Damn," said Melissa. "I'm sorry. I shouldn't have brought up the subject."

Karen stood, tugged at her shorts, and adjusted her T-shirt. "That's okay. I have to learn to be able to handle these things. But let's not talk about it anymore. We've made about five miles so far today. Not bad for two out-of-shape women who haven't biked in a while. But maybe it's time to head back."

Chapter 52

Karen hurried to find her sunglasses in the foggy darkness. She had to find them, it was urgent. She groped her way from room to room, feeling for drawer handles. Whose house was this? Oh . . . not hers . . .

She was dreaming, she realized, in that half-state between sleep and wakefulness where you can choose to go forward or back. She decided to drift, not get up, languish in laziness.

Beautiful one, you love to sleep in, don't you?

Her eyes flew open. That voice. Here in her bedroom. She sat up, looked around. He was sitting on the love seat under the window, smiling at her in this room where the light seemed so odd just now. She was not seeing in color or black-and-white. All was in sepia tones, browns, and yellows, almost as though she'd found the sunglasses in her dream and put them on.

"You!" Ari hadn't appeared to her since the night of Drew's emergency, and until just now, she'd pushed all thoughts of the visions from her mind. How had that been possible?

Yes, me. I've waited a long time, Karen. Can we talk?

He spoke like they were old friends getting together after a long absence. A wave of intense irritation washed over her. *Who did he think he was, to walk in and out of her life like this!*

"Can we talk? About what? Haven't you noticed you're dead?"

He patted the space beside him on the loveseat. *Why don't you get up, put on your robe, and come join me here? I think you have much to say to me too.*

"You arrogant son of a bitch," Karen sputtered. "I've been talking to you for two damned years in my head! I'm trying to get rid of you, not let you in further!"

It's getting closer to three years, isn't it?

Karen stared in disbelief. The man was unflappable! "Okay, I give up. Say your piece." She reached for her robe, wrapped and tied it around herself, and settled on the edge of the bed. Damned if he was going to instruct her every move!

Well, Karen . . . we didn't have enough time to say everything we needed to say. I've wanted to speak before . . . oh, have I wanted to . . . but you haven't been receptive until now.

Her mind flashed back to all the times—too many to count—catching a fleeting glimpse of him—gone when she turned to look. Was this the explanation? Aloud she said, "Receptive?"

Ari shrugged. *Perhaps "ready" is a better word. We have lots to talk about, Karen, but let's start with the pressing issues . . . our children.*

"Yes, indeed our children! And how they have suffered as a result of your actions, Ari!"

The smile left his face and he hung his head.

Damn him! How did he still have the power to make her feel guilty? "I suppose I have to accept some responsibility. I should have seen the signs with Drew. I should have been more help to Jocelyn when she was struggling with school."

He looked up again, his eyes focusing on hers. *One of the things I regret the most, Karen, is that I didn't have the opportunity to sit down with the kids and explain myself. Jocelyn seems to have comprehended without explanation. She's a survivor, she'll find her way. But Drew could have used my help. Drew keeps his thoughts and feelings inside. Fortunately, nothing irreparable has happened. You all have a chance now, to start fresh. You're closer to our children now than you've been in three years. You have great strength, Karen. Never forget that.*

He was right. She was strong. She'd found her strength as Drew lay unconscious in the hospital. She'd spent almost three years, a quivering mass, letting events happen to her. But when Drew was in the hospital, something had happened to change that, and she could almost name the moment. "You're right, Ari, I do. Better to find it late than not at all, I suppose."

The gentle smile returned to his face. *It was temporarily misplaced, not lost. And there are other things you have temporarily misplaced too. In a way, I took them from you. Now I want to make sure you get them back . . . I cannot leave this world otherwise. Let me help you find them, Karen.*

Karen's eyebrows scrunched in confusion. "You can't leave otherwise?"

Oh, I could. But I choose not to.

Karen's hands flew up in exasperation. "I see. I need help. So what is it you think I need help with?"

Ari shrugged. *What makes you angry with me? Specifically.*

She looked at him in disbelief and rose to her feet. "What? What, you ask?" She raked one hand through her hair as she looked wildly around the room.

Everything was still such a strange color. Kind of like an old yellowed photograph. How could he ask that? He must know. Okay, she'd spell it out.

"Betrayal!" The volume of her own voice shocked her. The word reverberated off the walls. When she caught her breath again, she continued. "You bastard, I was faithful to you for twenty years! Raised your kids, kept your house, fixed your meals"—by now, Karen was pacing back and forth in front of the love seat, gesturing wildly with one arm and holding her robe together with the other—"I was at your beck and call, and how did you repay me? You fucked around with men behind my back, expected me to believe you didn't know you were gay, humiliated me in front of the whole world! And then, you thought I should say, 'Delighted you found yourself, my dear husband.' Shit!" She sat on the bed again, this time at the foot.

You're entitled to say that, and there's nothing you can say that shouldn't be said. Just two corrections though. First, there was only ever one man. Adrian. And second, I truly did not know I was gay. In retrospect, perhaps I should have. But when we met, I thought I was straight, and I was happy with you and wanted to be a good husband and father. Those were my priorities in life, believe it or not.

"Right. I'm sure you were thinking about that when you were fucking Adrian." Karen's voice was calmer, but her words prickled with icy sarcasm.

Karen, what I need you to know is, it was nothing I planned. My plan was always for us. When Adrian came along, well, I couldn't help myself. I fell in love with him, and he with me. And out of that love came our physical desire. And the first time we were together, I knew.

"Knew what? Sexual ecstasy? That you didn't have with me?"

Ari's face was pained. *Yes. That's true. What I had with you, Karen, was special. But—*

Karen interrupted coldly. "But didn't measure up. Right?" By his silence, Karen knew the answer. She leaped to her feet and strode toward the love seat. Ari stood, facing her.

"You bastard! What does that make me? Some kind of a sexual nothing? Not enough woman for you! Not enough passion for you! So you go out and find your great passion! But what about me? What about the passion I never had? You big fuck!"

Out of control, she began to pummel his chest with her fists. "Now here I am, veins popping out on my arms and legs, sagging breasts, my waist is no longer twenty-five inches, and my hips—forget it! Well, past the age where I'm ever going to find the passion I deserved in life. But you found what you wanted and took it! Damn you, Ari Antilla!"

Exhausted, she collapsed into his chest sobbing. She could feel his arms around her, and a warmth that radiated and soothed like heated massage oil. Gradually, her muscles relaxed, and a calmness settled over her. She took a deep breath then exhaled slowly as she took a step back to separate from him.

His arms dropped to his side as she withdrew. He motioned for her to sit on the love seat. This time, she did, on the right-hand side where he indicated. In silence, he took his place next to her.

She turned to face him. "I've hated you, you know."

He nodded, his eyes narrowed in understanding. *You had a right. I won't argue with you about how you feel, except for one thing. Karen, you're an attractive woman.*

He raised his hand to touch her hair. *You still have your beautiful dark wavy hair and your lovely porcelain complexion. You blush, like a shy teenager—incredibly appealing—the mischief in your eyes is proof of your spirit! People always said Jocelyn took after me, but they were wrong. That mischievous streak came from you.*

At that, Karen had to laugh, remembering her antics in younger days. Oh, the fun they had when they were young. A wave of regret crept in, and she sighed. "Forty-five years old. My youth is gone."

Dearest, the spirit is still there if you want it. If only you could see my picture of you, a look of pure joy on your face, a wink in your eye, your graceful limbs ready to dance, always moving to the beat of your natural rhythm. You're a dancer, Karen, meant to enjoy not only the dance, but life. That's how I see you.

She looked at him cautiously. "You almost sound like you're still in love with me," she said quietly.

I always was, and I always will be. Never doubt that. Every loving word I said to you, every loving act, was totally true. Discovering I was gay did not change how I felt about you.

Karen was confused. "But, you wanted Adrian in your life, not me. It was Adrian you loved at the end."

It's true I loved Adrian, and that I'm gay, but, Karen, I never stopped loving you. My physical love for Adrian was stronger, yes. That's how I knew I was gay. But the love and affection I felt for you never changed. Can you understand?

She didn't know what to think. This was news. She'd always assumed he fell out of love with her when he fell in love with Adrian. "I don't know if I can or not," she answered. "All I know is, I've got boxes of photographs about a life, our life. And now I can't take any of the pictures out. Can't bear to see them because . . . well, I thought because—"

Because they aren't valid anymore? That Adrian changed all that?

She hesitated. "Well, yes, I guess that's it. I suppose . . ."

Yes?

"I suppose that's something like Drew was thinking, from what his psychiatrist said. He thinks if you and I shouldn't have been, then he shouldn't have been. But that is so far from the truth. I know that about the kids. I guess it would be the same for me too. All those years . . . they did count . . . for all of us."

Exactly. That is exactly what I want you all to know.

"Oh, Ari. It feels so good to talk to you like this. I never dreamed I'd have a chance." Karen's face clouded over as she remembered something. "Ari, about the end . . ."

He was on his feet now, pulling her toward the bed.

"At the hospital . . ."

He pulled the covers aside, gently pushed her into a sitting position.

She understood. He wanted her to go back to bed. She cooperated, but still tried to finish her sentence as he tucked the sheets around her. "At the hospital, Ari, when I left . . . I never said—"

Hush, beautiful, you can tell me good-bye when you see yourself as I picture you. That will be the time. Close your eyes Karen and rest.

She did as she was told, closed her eyes, and drifted on a gentle pillow, ocean waves quietly lapping as the sun rose on the horizon.

*   *   *

She opened her eyes. No Ari. She was alone in her bedroom. She leaped from her bed and dashed to the window to open the drapes. Outside, on the lawn, she noticed Igor languishing in the sunshine. She turned to scrutinize her room in the full brilliant morning color. *Could it have been a dream?* Didn't feel like it. She looked down at herself, and noticed she was still wearing her robe.

CHAPTER 53

"I guess we're not as good as we thought we were. Maybe we should stick to the old familiar bike path for a while." Karen paused to wipe her dripping face with a tissue as she and Melissa took a break at a picnic table.

Melissa tried in vain to fluff damp hair with her fingers. "Oh, what the hell. We can't always take the easy path."

Karen fanned herself with a bike glove. "Can't remember the last time I took an easy path." She took a swallow of water.

Melissa patted her hips excitedly. "Guess what? I've lost five pounds. I know you can't see it yet, but it feels good."

"Hey, that's great. I think I've lost about the same. Say, Melissa, can I bend your ear for a few minutes?"

"Go for it. I'm happy to sit here in the shade for a while. My legs feel like rubber."

Karen sucked in her breath. "All right, here goes." She cautiously explained Ari's late-night visit. When she was finished, Melissa's eyes were wide.

"Oh, that's eerie."

Karen shook her head. "Yes, it was one wild night. And I don't know how to explain it."

"You've been under a lot of stress. Everything happening with Drew and Jocelyn, not to mention work. Stress can play tricks with the mind."

"Normally that's what I'd think too, but this really is different. It has certainly caused me to do some thinking." Karen studied her fingernails.

"Did it happen or not? Was it really Ari? It felt real." She returned her gaze to Melissa. "When I touched him, he was warm. I pounded on his chest, and it was hard. He held me, and I felt pressure. His green eyes twinkled as they always had. I can't believe I'm telling you this. You must wonder if I'm losing it."

"Oh, it's definitely strange. No doubt about that. But let's say Ari was there. What then?"

"Much of what he said made sense. He was right, I was so consumed with anger and grief, I wouldn't have been receptive before. I hope I'm doing better now."

Melissa reached across the table to touch Karen's hand. "You are, Karen," she said gently. "Give yourself some credit."

Karen shook her head, blinking back tears. "I wasted more than two years being bitter and blaming. God, how did that help? Look what happened to Drew. I hurt him. How can I forgive myself? And Jocelyn, I almost lost her as a daughter because I couldn't understand and accept her as she was."

"Karen, you can't go back and undo what's happened."

Suddenly Ari's words came back.

Nothing irreparable has happened. You all have a chance now, to start fresh.

"Yes, you're right, Melissa. I'm really going to try to do things differently. For myself and for Drew and Jocelyn. In fact, right now I've decided I'm going to phone Jocelyn and tell her I'd like to take her and Lisa to lunch."

Melissa was incredulous. "Am I hearing you right? Jocelyn *and* Lisa?"

"Yes," Karen said firmly. "Things I can do nothing about, I just have to accept. I want a fresh start, a new page, with Jocelyn. If she cares about Lisa, she must be a special person. And I'll look for that in her too."

"I don't believe I'm saying this, Karen, but it sounds like Ari's words have helped."

Karen nodded. "And, Melissa, an amazing thing is, I'm feeling his love more strongly than his betrayal for the first time since he told me about Adrian."

Every loving word I said to you, every loving act, was totally true. Discovering I was gay did not change how I felt about you.

"You're talking about Ari as if he's still here!"

Karen voice was slow and measured. "Well, maybe he is. He told me he couldn't say good-bye until I saw myself as he saw me, and I really don't understand what that means. But some time I know it will all become clear."

CHAPTER 54

When the meeting ended, Grace followed Drew out the door. She raked her blonde hair back with one hand as she spoke. "Hey, Drew, are you in a big hurry to go home?"

Drew often walked the short distance from his grandmother's house to the campus AA meetings. Good exercise, fresh air, he figured. Today he hadn't been in the mood for AA, but seeing Grace in the room had improved his outlook.

"No, I'm not in a rush," he replied. "Do you want to walk around campus for a while?"

Grace's voice was jovial as they turned down Adams Street. "I was surprised to see you at the meeting tonight. It's my home group, you know."

Drew zipped his pale yellow windbreaker, surprised at the drop in temperature since sunset. "No, I didn't know, but it was nice to see a familiar face. I've tried a few different meeting times. My counselor wants me to go once a week minimum, twice a week is better. Maybe from now on, I'll come to this one."

Grace seemed to glide as she walked, her hair floating behind. It was the same way she had moved when she danced with him the night of the party. Remembering the fragrance of her hair, he wished he could lean over and smell it now.

A serious expression came over Grace's face. "There's something I've been wanting to tell you."

He glanced in her direction and hoped his smile didn't look strained. "Go ahead."

She spoke in a monotone, not meeting his glance. "Colin and I broke up."

So that was it. He felt numb. "Oh, too bad." He knew that probably sounded pretty lame. Hopefully, she hadn't noticed the break in his voice.

They walked several steps in silence. Looking at the sidewalk, he remembered the old game step on a crack, break your mother's back. He always tried not to step on cracks.

"It was pretty much over by the time we visited you in the hospital, for me anyway," Grace explained. "I realized it was foolish of me to continue going out with Colin."

"Oh yeah?" Drew tried to keep his voice noncommittal.

"Yeah. Because, well, because I always wanted to go out with you."

The numb feeling persisted. "That's what you told me in the hospital. But you had a funny way of showing it." Maybe he should just shut up.

Grace continued as if she hadn't heard him. "I called you several times, remember, and you always had some excuse. I finally thought, to hell with it, I'll see if Colin wants to go out. Just to hurt you. Because you hurt me. It all seems so stupid now." She kicked a stone that was lying on the sidewalk. It flew several feet ahead.

Drew, still avoiding cracks, noticed the stone, and kicked it further along.

Grace kicked the stone again before she slowed down, reached for Drew's arm, and turned to look at him as she walked. "But Colin wasn't you, Drew. After I got the DUI and got sober, I did some thinking."

Drew kicked the stone again. This time it flew into the street. Gone. What would she do if he reached for her hand and held it? The hand that was on his arm.

"I don't know what to say."

Grace wrapped her arm tighter around his. "I'm not finished. I knew I had to break up with Colin. We weren't right."

Drew felt the pressure of her hand on his arm. He said in a flat voice, "I don't know if I should say I'm sorry or not."

Grace said with conviction, "I'm not sorry. It's the best thing. I saw that clearly after I stopped drinking. When I drank, I thought I was the life of the party." She threw her head back and laughed. "Ha. Me, Grace, social butterfly. I could talk to people then. Like you, at the party the night we met."

Grace released his arm from her grasp. Drew hesitantly reached out and took her hand in his. She didn't pull her hand away.

"You talked easily to me that night for sure." Drew's hand began to sweat. The numbness was receding.

Grace squeezed his hand and winked. "It was alcohol talking. And you were the sober one."

He smirked. "Yeah, the responsible designated driver. To take Colin home. Should've stayed responsible. Everything went to hell after that."

She squeezed his hand again. "For me too, in a different way. Finding out you were in the hospital hit me hard. I wondered if I was responsible. By dating Colin."

Drew stopped walking, turned toward Grace, and took her other hand. "No, of course not. Put that idea out of your mind."

Grace met his gaze, biting her lip. "Good, I worried about that." She let go of his right hand, and they started to walk again. Her voice lightened. "Have you been back to talk to your advisor yet?"

"No, I haven't. Been thinking about it though. Guess I should make myself walk into his office on campus tomorrow, but I'm nervous about what he'll say. I flunked that math test pretty bad."

"Tell him the truth," she said simply.

There was a short silence as Drew contemplated Grace's words. She was so easy to talk with.

"You're probably right. I'll let you know. I think I should head back to Granbo's. I'll walk you to your apartment first." His hand wasn't sweating anymore.

"All right, it's getting a bit cool anyway. Wish I'd worn a jacket."

Drew looked down at his windbreaker, feeling guilty it hadn't occurred to him to offer it to her. "I'm sorry. Would you like to borrow mine?"

Grace smiled. "No, but thanks. We're almost there. I'll be fine. Oh, you said nothing too much is happening at your gram's house. I'm going sailing with Dad on Sunday for the first time this spring. He said I could invite a friend along, someone to help crew. Would you like to come?"

He looked at the sidewalk, shuffled his feet. "Thanks, but I'm not good at that kind of thing."

Grace persisted. "How do you know? Have you ever tried?"

"Nope. Never. Now, if I could just sit back and relax with my feet up, and a remote control . . ." He tried to make a joke.

She would have none of it. "Well, damn, it's not all that hard. You just have to be able to follow directions. My dad will teach you. He's good at telling people what to do." She giggled. "He'll also tell you he's been sailing since he was nine and even sailed on an America's Cup team in his twenties. You want to give it a try?"

Maybe if she persisted, he'd consider it.

He moved his left foot off the crack in the sidewalk.

"Just this once?" she pleaded.

"Okay. You've convinced me." He grinned shyly.

"Great, just in time too. Here's my apartment. Give me your gram's number, and I'll call you later in the week." She tightened her grip on his hand for a moment before letting go.

Chapter 55

Jocelyn spotted her mother's emerald green suit in the sea of black clothing inside the restaurant. Karen was seated at a window table on the far side of the room. Moving closer to Lisa, she whispered, "Sure you're ready for this?" Their eyes met as she took Lisa's hand, squeezing it briefly.

"Yes, I'm ready." Lisa's smile was strained, but Jocelyn could see that she was determined to go through with the meeting.

Karen caught sight of them and waved. Jocelyn was pleased to see a welcoming smile on her mother's face. As they approached the table, Karen rose, hugged Jocelyn and extended her hand to Lisa.

"So glad you could come, Lisa. I wanted a chance to meet you under less harried circumstances. The last time we met . . ." Karen's voice trailed off to an awkward silence.

Lisa nodded in understanding. "I know, Mrs. Antilla."

"Oh, please, Lisa. Call me Karen. That's a very pretty dress, by the way."

"Oh, thank you," said Lisa. As she seated herself, she smoothed the skirt of her teal two-piece spandex outfit.

Jocelyn looked from her well-dressed mother to a carefully attired Lisa and was suddenly conscious of her own outfit, too-loose Dockers, and a too-wrinkled plum-colored silk shirt.

In an effort to ignore her feelings of fashion inadequacy, Jocelyn glanced around. "Glad you suggested this restaurant for lunch, Mom. I love Bryant

Park. It's one of the refreshing spots of green in the middle of the concrete city. Haven't been here in ages. You always know the nicest places."

"Thanks, dear. I did live here for a few years myself, remember."

Jocelyn gave a feathery laugh. "Well, no, I don't remember. We moved shortly after I was born, didn't we?"

"Yes, that's right." Karen signaled the end of the subject by picking up the menu. "If I remember correctly, the salads here are excellent. And the sandwiches too."

After they ordered lunch, Karen quizzed Lisa about her family, her hobbies, and her job as a physical therapist. Lisa reciprocated with questions about the teaching profession and schoolchildren in general.

Jocelyn leaned back in her chair, listening intently as she sipped her iced tea. She couldn't have been more pleased. Her mother had come a long way since that weekend in January. Not only did she seem genuinely interested in Lisa, but at this moment, the two of them were as agreeable as tortilla chips and salsa. Jocelyn suspected Lisa might be more like the daughter her mother had hoped for than she was! Except for the gayness, of course.

The conversation finally turned Jocelyn's way shortly after the waiter served their lunches, a sandwich for Jocelyn and salads for her mother and Lisa.

"Do you see each other much at work?" Her mother looked directly at her, not mincing any words, as usual.

Jocelyn roused herself into speaking mode. "Not really. Our paths never cross, unless we arrange it. Totally different departments, nowhere near each other. It's a large hospital."

"Sometimes I stop by Jocelyn's department if I'm done early," added Lisa. "Not too often, though."

"I see," said Karen. "Jocelyn, you're actually going out on runs, now?"

"Yes. Primarily as an observer. Another student, Mike, and I have been assigned to the same unit."

Lisa chuckled. "Oh yes, Mike. I've met him. Great sense of humor, that guy."

Jocelyn nudged Lisa with her foot. "You've got that right. But you know, it's good to laugh on this job. You have to, as stressful as it is sometimes. And everybody likes Mike."

Lisa looked at Jocelyn teasingly. "I think Mike has a thing for you."

Jocelyn blushed. "Nah, he's just a friendly guy. Jokes with everyone."

Karen looked amused. "Does he know . . ." She hesitated for a moment and started again. "Does he know about the two of you?"

Jocelyn and Lisa exchanged glances before Jocelyn replied. "We haven't painted him a picture, Mom, but he'd have to be an idiot not to know. I talk about Lisa all the time."

Karen looked thoughtful. "Yes, I can see that you wouldn't go out of your way to announce your relationship at work. And it's nobody's business, anyway."

"Exactly," said Jocelyn. She grew prouder of her mother by the minute.

The waiter brought the bill, placing it in front of Karen. She gave him her credit card and continued talking.

"How are you liking the job, dear, now that you're seeing some action?"

Jocelyn beamed. "I just love it, Mom. It's so exciting to be able to help people. It's intense and physical. I love being useful. I'm right in my element."

Karen looked pleased. "I love to hear someone enthused about their job. That's more important than anything."

"Thanks, Mom. I agree. And I'm so grateful for the trust Grandfather Whittaker set up because otherwise, I couldn't afford to do this."

Karen nodded. "Yes, my dad always valued higher education, and both Drew and you have benefited. Not to change the subject, but have you spoken to Adrian lately?"

Jocelyn's mouth fell open. Would wonders never cease? Her mother, actually bringing up Adrian's name!

"Well, no, I haven't seen him much. But I've talked to him on the phone. Probably a couple of times in the last two weeks. Why?"

Karen sighed. "Oh, he phoned me a while back. Said he has something for me. Needs to deliver it in person. Do you know anything about this?"

Jocelyn shook her head. "No, Mom. That's weird. He hasn't said anything to me."

"Interesting," Karen mumbled.

"I'll see what I can find out, if you want," Jocelyn offered.

"Oh, that's okay. Don't worry about it."

Jocelyn said nothing, but she was puzzled. It was so unlikely that Adrian would ever call her mother. And how odd that Adrian hadn't mentioned the call to her.

Karen signed the bill, leaving a generous tip, put her credit card away, and looked at her watch. "Shall we take a stroll, girls, or do some shopping? I have a good two hours before the train."

"Sure, let's walk around," said Jocelyn, rising to her feet.

"I'll just go to the ladies' room for a moment if you don't mind," said Lisa.

"Okay, Mom and I will wait out front."

*   *   *

Jocelyn and Karen gazed out the foyer window enjoying the peaceful green of the park.

"Jocelyn, while I have the chance, I just want to mention what a fine young woman Lisa is. You may bring her home any time."

Jocelyn stared at her mother for a full thirty seconds, knowing they were both remembering the same shouted words. Her eyes welled. She wrapped her arms around her mother, burying her head in her shoulder.

"Thank you, Mom," she croaked. When she stepped back, she saw her tears mirrored in her mother's eyes.

"Mom, you know I never . . . about all those women . . . what I said . . . I never—"

Karen placed her forefinger lightly on Jocelyn's lips. "Hush, Jocelyn. I know. Despite your feisty nature, you've never been casual about a thing in your life."

CHAPTER 56

The sound of the doorbell jolted Drew from his Saturday morning television reverie. His grandmother peered around the doorway from the kitchen where she was having a cup of coffee and reading the morning newspaper.

"Why don't you get the door, hon. It's your mom. I see her car in the driveway."

"Sure, Granbo." He muted the television and shuffled across the living room to open the door.

"Hi, Mom. I figured you'd be here pretty early. Come on in."

His mother's quick hug felt good to him this morning. He hugged her back.

"Morning, son. Yup, I'm an early riser. You're looking good, TV on as usual," Karen teased. "Where's Helen?"

"Oh, Granbo's in the kitchen, Mom." The kitchen was Granbo's domain.

"Hi, Helen," Karen called out, loud enough to be heard in the other room.

His grandmother strode into the living room in a royal blue jumpsuit with heels to match, her fancy coffee cup in hand. "Oh, hi, Karen. I'm waiting for my client to arrive. Hadn't planned any appointments today, but June Halverson called yesterday in need of an emergency color. Her roots are showing, and she has a big to-do at the country club tonight. It won't take long. I wouldn't do it for just anyone, you know. Karen, I forgot to ask, do you want coffee?"

"Thanks. Not right now, Helen. Maybe later, if there's still some to be had."

"There's always coffee here, Karen. Oops, here's June. I know you came to talk to Drew anyway. I'll join you a little later." His grandmother walked toward the door that led into the salon.

Karen settled herself on the couch next to Drew. He wondered what she would want to talk about today. She seemed to have something on her mind.

"How are things going? Did you have a good week?"

He answered with what even he recognized as his stock response. "Everything's fine, Mom."

"I hope you mean what you're saying. We've got to be able to talk to each other, to tell the truth."

There's that word again. Truth. Drew rolled his eyes and smiled. "Funny, someone else just told me truth is the best way. Must be my lesson for the week."

"Glad to see a smile on your face." His mother readjusted a pillow on the sofa. "Say, last weekend I went to see Jocelyn. Had lunch with Lisa and her at the Bryant Park Café."

Drew raised an eyebrow. "With Lisa, too? I thought you—"

"Well, I've changed my mind. I've had time to do a lot of thinking. Jocelyn's happy. That's the important thing, and she's enjoying her job training. She's hoping to see you soon."

"I hope so. Last time I saw her . . ." He didn't finish his sentence. *Mom, Josey, and Lisa eating together. Talking. Smiling. Was this really his mom?*

"I know your sister will work something out. But I'm not here to talk about Jocelyn. You told me on the phone that you had some news. I'm all ears."

Leave it to his mom to get right to the point. She never was much into small talk. "I went to talk to my advisor on Thursday, and I have some good news. I didn't think I'd graduate after failing the test. Well, I found out my grade will be low, but I'll still pass. And the best part is, if I show them a letter from my doctor, they'll give me two years to retest if I want to improve my grade point average."

Karen's eyes danced. He knew she'd be excited. "What good news! I can't believe you didn't tell me this first thing. You'll graduate after all."

"Yes, I'll get my diploma even though I missed the ceremony. And there's one more thing. Are you ready for this?" Drew took a deep breath. "I made a decision. I'm not going to be a stockbroker. That was Dad, but it's not me.

I'm not cut out for sales." He prepared himself for the worst, annoyed with himself for hoping his mother would approve. It was his life.

"But, Drew, isn't it kind of late to change your mind?"

Darn, she was going to make it hard for him. He made an effort to keep his voice calm. "I'm not exactly changing my mind, Mom. I'm going to continue in school another year or so to get my master's. I want to do research, be an analyst rather than a broker. My advisor thinks this is a workable plan."

"Research, I never thought about that, but I can see you in that field." His mother's eyes lit up as she spoke. She did understand!

For the next ten minutes, his mother listened as he outlined his plan to continue in school. Karen leaned back. "My goodness, you children are full of surprises lately. How can I keep up with all these changes?"

He wasn't the only one. "I think you're changing, too, Mom."

Karen flashed him smile and went to the kitchen to have some of Helen's coffee.

Drew tossed the remote up and down absently while waiting for his mother to return. He'd better tell her his other news. "There's one more thing. I hope the weather warms up because I'm going sailing tomorrow."

Karen took a sip of coffee. She grimaced. "Gosh, strong coffee." She set the cup down then looked up in surprise. "Sailing? You don't know how to sail."

"You're right, Mom, but I'm going to learn. I know this girl, her name is Grace."

CHAPTER 57

H elen breezed into the room with her usual aplomb, Karen observed as she finished her coffee.

"Well, I've got her fixed up for tonight. Couldn't let one of my clients go out with her roots showing." Helen took a breath. "Now I can relax for a minute. More coffee, Karen? I see your cup's empty."

Helen disappeared into the kitchen, not waiting for an answer.

"No thanks," Karen murmured. She turned to Drew. "Wonder what she would have done if I'd said yes?"

They both chuckled.

"You know Granbo." Drew shook his head. "She's like the Energizer bunny, doesn't stop for anything." His fondness for his grandmother was obvious.

Helen returned with an ice-filled highball glass and a straw. "Coffee was too old, anyway." She seated herself in the elegant New England Queen Anne chair, which suited her perfectly.

"Did Drew tell you he's going sailing tomorrow?" Helen shot the remark in Karen's direction without looking at her.

"Yes, he sure did. Sounds like a wonderful opportunity." Karen was irritated, but she tried to keep her voice nonchalant. Her mother-in-law seldom looked directly at her.

"I'll say. I know the family," said Helen as she stirred the ice in her glass. "Wealthy folk. I do Roseanne Van Gilder's hair. That's Grace's mother. She's due in here next week sometime."

"Interesting," said Karen stiffly. She wasn't impressed. Helen loved to talk about her uppity clients. "I'm sure Drew will have a nice time."

"Yes, I'm sure he will," Helen replied in a dry, flat tone.

An uncomfortable silence ensued. Karen tried to think of a safe subject but failed. Drew was the first to speak.

"Fourth of July is next week, isn't it?" His words hung in the air.

Helen stared at him a moment. "Yes, it is."

"Remember when we all used to get together for a picnic? Every year we did that. Until . . ."

"That's right." Karen's tone was cautious. She didn't like the direction this conversation was going.

"Wouldn't it be nice . . ." Drew flushed as the eyes of both women fixed on him. He continued. "Well, I just thought, maybe we could do it again."

"Oh, no, impossible. I have plans," Helen stated without hesitation.

Karen was flustered. "Well, I . . . no, Drew, I don't think it would work. Jocelyn's schedule . . ."

"That's right," agreed Helen, interrupting. "Jocelyn's schedule. No, wouldn't work."

How dare Helen think she could command every action! Karen glared at her. "It might work," she said icily. "After all, we don't know Jocelyn's schedule. We'd have to ask."

Helen glared back, fire in her eyes. "True. But we know my schedule, and I'm already committed. So that's that."

Karen was furious. What an imperious woman! "Damn it, Helen, I can't believe you can sit there and lie. I doubt you have anything going on. You just damned well don't want to be in my company, and that's the truth of it!"

Helen raised herself taller in her chair, giving Karen her full venom. "How dare you suggest I'm lying! Of course, I have plans! After all, you don't bother to extend invitations to me for these holiday things! What do you want me to do, sit around by myself?"

Karen couldn't believe what she was hearing. "I don't extend invitations? Well, of course not! Not anymore! Was I supposed to keep asking you so you could snub me every time? And where, may I ask, were your invitations to me? Oh, sure, the kids are always welcome here, but not me! You've made that crystal clear!"

Drew stood. "Mom, Granbo, hold on."

Both women ignored him.

Helen rose to her feet. "Honestly, Karen. What an imagination you have."

Karen stood as well, noting that she had to look up to Helen. It was those damned high heels! "Imagination? No way. I know exactly what you think of me, and I know exactly why. Damn it, Helen, I can't change what I did or why I did it!"

Suddenly, Drew put his hands over his ears and yelled at the top of his lungs. "Stop! Do you hear me? Stop, now!"

Drew's words reverberated in the room. He was uncharacteristically red in the face. His hands were shaking. Neither Helen nor Karen had witnessed him in such a rage before. He looked back and forth between the two women, speaking in a strong voice that left no doubt what he thought. "Can't you see what you are doing to our family by keeping up this vendetta against each other? There's only four of us left now that Dad's gone, and we need each other. *I need all of you*, and I need you to get along. Today, tomorrow, and every day, from here on. Everyone wants to help me. Well, damn it, *this* is how you can help me. Pull together for a change!"

For a moment, Karen couldn't believe what was happening. She stood with her mouth open. Finally, the words came. "Drew," she stammered, "of course we'll do that. We're all here for you. Aren't we, Helen?" She prayed that Helen would see what they needed to do, for Drew's sake.

"Yes, for sure," Helen replied faintly.

Thank God she did.

When she spoke again, Helen's voice was gentle. "Drew, are you okay?"

Out of energy, Drew sat down. "Yes, Granbo, I'm fine. Just need to calm down a bit. But I'm not kidding, I want you and Mom to resolve your problems, and I want us to start acting like a family again." Once more, he looked from one to the other.

Helen was the first to speak. "Yes," she said energetically. "We can do it. I can do it." She turned to Karen. "It's over, Karen. I don't like what you did when my Ari was dying, but what you say is true. It's impossible to go back and change it."

Finally, Helen had spoken the truth. Karen hardly knew what to say, but she had to say something. "Yes, Helen, I agree. It's over. I'm willing if you are."

Helen's eyes met Karen's. "I only need to know one thing, and then I'll put it out of my mind forever."

"What's that?" Karen was cautious, dreading what the question might be.

"If you could go back and do it differently, might you have stayed, for Ari?"

Karen felt a combination of relief and fatigue. This was not the question she'd expected, but one she'd asked herself often. She sighed wearily. "You know, Helen, I couldn't admit this until just recently, but I'll tell you. Yes, I've had regrets, but at the time, I just couldn't do it any other way. Do you understand?"

Helen continued to look steadily into Karen's eyes. "No, to be truthful, I don't, but at least you had regrets. That means something to me. I'm willing to put it behind us."

Karen's back stiffened. "And so am I, for all of our sakes." She hoped Helen meant what she said.

Helen turned to Drew. "We'll go on as a family again. Complete with each other and whomever any of us should happen to choose as a companion. From now on, your mother and I will get along."

"Yes, we will," Karen said with conviction.

Helen frowned. "But, I do have something to tell you both. I really do have a commitment on the Fourth of July. That wasn't a lie. If I'd known you wanted us all to be together, Drew, I wouldn't have made that arrangement. But in the future, all holidays will be reserved as family occasions, starting with Labor Day! How does that sound?"

Drew grinned sheepishly. "Sounds great. Thanks, Mom. Granbo. Sorry for yelling. I didn't know I was going to do that."

Karen hugged her son. "Well, Drew, I think it's about time you shouted."

"Definitely," agreed Helen. "Better to let it out a bit at a time, no good letting it fester."

Karen turned to Helen, deciding to make a peace offering. "What say we all go out for lunch?"

"Nice idea," said Helen. "I know just the place."

Of course, you do, thought Karen. *You know everything. But in spite of that, we're going to get along!*

CHAPTER 58

Turning sideways, Karen surveyed herself in the full-length mirror in the master bedroom. Not bad. Her ten-pound weight loss was showing. She hadn't been able to wear these shorts in years.

Pleased with herself, she decided to prune a few roses in the garden before Melissa arrived for their usual Saturday afternoon bike ride. A little bending and twisting might do even more for her figure.

Retrieving her gardening gloves, a pair of pruning sheers, and a plastic sack from the garage, she went to the front yard and began to clip back the dead blooms. True, she had a yardman, but he seldom got around to her roses. And no one could do the job as well as she could.

Pruning roses always brought back memories of her parents and their love of flowers, especially roses. Although she was their only child, she couldn't remember either of her parents working outside the home. Her father, CEO of the accounting firm started by her grandfather, had retired several years before she was born. While they were alive, she'd had the benefit of their time, patience, and wealth. The downside was that they had died when she was a young woman, still in her twenties. She had no aunts, uncles or cousins. Her only blood relatives were her children.

Karen wondered if she and her children would have found it easier when Ari died if they'd had more family to lean on. She regretted that Jocelyn and Drew had never known her parents, although compared to Helen, she was certain they would have considered them stuffy.

"Ouch!" Karen stood, pulled off a glove and put her middle finger in her mouth. A thorn had stabbed her right through the glove. She took her finger from her mouth and inspected it. It wasn't bleeding; she'd live.

At that moment, she heard the sound of a car on the gravel driveway. *Melissa must be early,* she thought as she turned around. But it wasn't Melissa's car. It was a black Audi. *Who on earth? Oh my. Adrian.*

She pulled the other glove off and watched as he pulled the car up, killed the engine, and climbed out. How did the man always manage to look like he'd stepped out of a magazine ad, she wondered, as she noted his perfectly pressed gray pants and elegant turquoise sweater.

Suddenly, the door on the passenger side opened, and Jocelyn emerged. "Jocelyn! I wasn't expecting you."

Her daughter sprinted the short distance across the lawn and hugged her while Adrian hung back in the driveway, waiting.

"I know you weren't, Mom." Jocelyn's eyes were wide with excitement. "But I called Adrian the other day to ask about that stuff you mentioned at lunch, and when I realized it was something that couldn't be mailed, I decided we should deliver it today. If you weren't home, I figured I could just put it in the house and leave a note."

Adrian's mouth fell open. "I thought you asked your mother."

Jocelyn blushed. "I, uh, may have stretched the truth a bit, Adrian. I didn't exactly tell Mom we were coming."

Adrian and Karen both stared at her intently. Finally, Jocelyn turned to her mother. "Sorry, Mom," she said weakly.

Karen was annoyed. She could see that Adrian was embarrassed, which in an odd way, pleased her. She decided to keep her thoughts to herself rather than say anything to Jocelyn, since they had been getting along so well lately.

"Oh, it's fine, I guess, but Melissa will be here in . . ." she looked at her watch, "about forty-five minutes for our bike ride."

"Don't worry, we're not staying, just dropping off and leaving. I'm on shift at four o'clock." Jocelyn stepped back, and eyed her mother. "Mom, you're looking good! Your bike riding is paying off!"

Karen flushed. "Thanks," she said self-consciously, wishing Jocelyn wouldn't talk about her appearance in front of Adrian.

But Adrian wasn't looking at her. He had opened the rear door and was pulling out a large flat box that took up most of the space between the car floor and ceiling. She wondered how he'd been able to see anything in the rear-view mirror.

"What on earth . . . ?" she asked aloud, her voice trailing off.

"Jocelyn, if you'll give me a hand to the door," said Adrian, "I think you and your mother can handle it from there."

Jocelyn complied, and the pair maneuvered their way from the car up the three steps to the front door as Karen followed, digging in her pocket for the key. When Adrian and Jocelyn reached the porch, they set the box down.

"It's really not all that heavy. More awkward than anything," Adrian advised. "Jocelyn, take as much time as you want. I'll be sitting in the car with my book. No hurry."

Karen was grateful for Adrian's sensitivity. In no way did she want that man to set foot in her house.

"Let's drag it into the family room, Mom," said Jocelyn, taking charge.

The box was open on the top, allowing Karen to take a peek. "What is it, some kind of painting?"

"Yes, that's what Adrian said," muttered Jocelyn. "Here, I'll hold the sides of it, and you pull the box away."

They carefully removed several layers of paper, working from the back of the painting. When they had finished, the two women turned the painting around, stepping back to view it.

Karen gasped, putting a hand to her mouth. The painting revealed a dark-haired, animated woman in a low cut rose-colored chiffon dress. The woman was in the act of twirling so that the skirt flared out dramatically, one arm flung high in the air, the other holding a single delicate red rose.

"Mom, it's you, dancing!" Jocelyn said.

Not taking her eyes off the painting, Karen staggered backward until she found the sofa behind her. She sat down in an effort to steady herself as Ari's words came back to her.

You're a dancer, Karen, meant to enjoy not only the dance but life.

She swallowed, blinking hard to keep the tears from coming, but it was useless. They overflowed the moment she tried to speak.

"But, who . . . how . . . ?"

The words wouldn't come. Fortunately, Jocelyn understood. She sat next to her mom, putting an arm around her shoulder.

"I know, Mom. This was to be Dad's Christmas present to you two years ago. I guess the artist had been working on it for ages, but it wasn't finished until after Dad died."

"But, did you know . . ." Again, Karen ran out of words, and again, Jocelyn comprehended.

"No, I hadn't seen the painting. Adrian hasn't either. It's been kept in that box since the artist delivered it."

"The artist, who *is* the artist?"

Jocelyn studied the bottom of the painting. "Jackson Nederby. Anyone you know?"

Karen nodded as tears ran soundlessly down her cheeks. "Yes, I've seen his work and admired it. Your father knew. But, I never thought . . ."

"Mom, it's beautiful. You're beautiful. At first, it reminded me of when you were younger. Remember how you and Dad would disco dance in the living room? You were both so good. But now that I look closer, it's not when you were younger. It's you. Now. But dancing like you used to, with that same look on your face. It tickles me. You look so . . ." She struggled for the right word. "Alive."

At that, the dam burst. "Alive! Yes, damn it, that's what I am. Alive!" She sobbed hard in her daughter's arms. The tears that hadn't come at the funeral finally flowed like lava down the sides of a volcano.

CHAPTER 59

"Mom, I'm so sorry," said Jocelyn. "This has all been so hard on you."

"I guess I'm being rather emotional," said Karen. "Sorry."

"Don't be, Mom. I think the tears are good for you."

"Oh, Jocelyn, on top of everything else, something awful happened this week. Igor is gone."

"What?" asked Jocelyn, stunned.

"Yes. The Wilsons boarded him at the Animal Care Clinic when they went on their weeklong vacation. When they returned to pick him up, the manager told them that they had accidentally given Igor, in his close-sided pet carrier, to the wrong person, and that person, upon getting home and discovering it was not her own cat, threw Igor out the back door!"

"You've got to be kidding," Jocelyn said, shocked. "What kind of person would do that? I'm just sick about this! Where did that woman live?"

"About two miles away. The Wilsons have put an ad in the local paper, and they've put up signs in the woman's neighborhood, but no sign of him."

"This is absolutely terrible. I'm going over to the Wilsons right now to see if there is anything I can do. I love that cat!"

"I know, honey, we all do. I'm sad to say it doesn't look promising."

"We can't give up hope, Mom."

"You're right. We can't."

Jocelyn headed next door, and Karen returned to the family room to study her portrait, tears running down her cheeks. Moments later, the doorbell rang. Karen had lost track of time. She opened the door to find Melissa on the porch in biking attire.

"Hey, you don't look ready," Melissa said.

"It's Adrian. He's here. And Jocelyn too." Karen dabbed at her eyes with a tissue, nodded in the direction of the driveway. "Did you notice his car? I won't be able to go today."

The smile faded from Melissa's face. "You've been crying. Are you okay?"

"I'll be fine. Really I will." Karen blew her nose. "Can we bike tomorrow instead?"

"Sure, same time tomorrow works. I'll take a short ride myself and then head home."

"Great, I appreciate that. See you tomorrow."

Karen stood at the open door as her friend pedaled down the street. Her gaze shifted to Adrian's car. He sat with his window rolled down, reading a book. With quiet determination, she closed the door then walked toward the Audi. "Can we talk for a few minutes?"

Adrian folded over the corner of his page. "Yes, of course. The door's open," he said waving in the direction of the passenger seat. "Come on in."

Karen climbed into the car, tissues still in hand.

"I'm sorry, Karen. I don't know what to say."

Karen sensed that Adrian almost reached out to touch her in a comforting gesture but then reconsidered.

She dabbed at her eyes again. "I'll be okay. The painting was a surprise, a shock. I had no idea the gift from Ari would be something like this."

"He wished it had been done earlier so he could have given it to you himself. I've had it for almost two years. I wouldn't have felt right opening it, though I must admit I was curious. I did cut open the top of the box to make it easier for you to remove it, but you're the first person besides the artist to see it."

"Yes, Jocelyn told me," Karen sighed. "It's a beautiful painting. Thank you for taking good care of it for me. I don't think I'd have been ready to see it before now."

"Well, sometimes things work out as they should. We can always be thankful when that happens."

"As long as we're here, there's something I've wanted to ask you." Karen bit her lip and continued, "Adrian, what would have happened if Ari had lived?" Her voice was almost a whisper. "I mean, was he planning to leave me?"

Adrian looked thoughtful. "I'll tell you what I know." He reached over and touched Karen's arm briefly. "Ari never said anything about leaving you. He loved you."

"That confuses me. In fact, it doesn't make sense."

"Karen, he was tortured by conflicting feelings and guilt. He felt a sense of commitment to you and the children. Then he got sick, and he told me that if you felt you had to leave him, he'd understand. But it wouldn't be his choice."

"Adrian, if you knew that Ari was married, why did you . . . ?" Sobbing again, Karen couldn't finish the question.

"Sometimes it just isn't that easy. I loved him, but I felt divided too. I'd be lying if I said that I know what the future would have been if Ari had lived."

Karen was quiet for a few minutes, remembering the dinner when Ari had told her about his cancer. She glanced at Adrian who appeared to be lost in his own thoughts.

Finally he spoke again. "I'd said good-bye to Ari before he went to the hospital that last time. He knew, and I knew, that he wouldn't come home. It was the hardest thing I've ever done. I knew I wouldn't be able to be with him in the end. That was your place, Karen."

Karen was stunned. "What do you mean, you said good-bye before he went to the hospital? Ari asked for you, and you came. I gave permission."

"He asked for me, but not for the reason you thought. He'd forgotten to tell me about the picture, the picture I brought to you today. The artist hadn't finished it yet. He asked me to make sure you got it. I promised him I would."

"My god, if only I had known!"

"I couldn't tell you anything then. I promised Ari. He wanted it to be a surprise."

"I've never really thought about how hard Ari's death was for you too. Not only for me and the children. You lost someone too. I don't know if I'll ever be able to say these words again, Adrian, but I'm truly sorry for your loss."

"And I'm sorry for yours, Karen. It's been hard for all of us, but I think at last we're finding our way."

CHAPTER 60

It was a sunny but breezy June day, perfect for bike riding. Returning from an hour on the tree-lined parkway near her home, Karen rounded the corner as Drew walked up the front sidewalk. He looked startled to see her.

"Mom, I can't remember the last time I saw you on a bike." He grinned. "You look like you're having fun."

Karen's eyes twinkled as her mouth stretched into a broad smile. She jumped off the bike and gave Drew a hug and a peck on the cheek before answering. "I'm definitely having fun, Drew. So much fun that I think I'll have to buy my own bike instead of borrowing Jocelyn's."

"I remember Josey's bike. How often do you ride?" he asked, touching the handlebars gently.

"Almost every day since school let out. Just took a little morning ride with Melissa. Glad I got back here in time. Come on, let's go in the house through the garage so I can put this bike away." She took a remote from her pocket to raise the garage door.

"Good to see you getting out like this," Drew said as they entered the house. His tone was sincere, but the look on his face was one of faint disbelief. "Any news about Igor? Josey told me."

Karen sighed. "No, not yet. The Wilsons are heartbroken. In fact, the whole neighborhood is distraught."

Drew shook his head. "Poor little guy. I hope he's safe, wherever he is."

"Only so much we can do," said Karen as she unzipped her light jacket and tossed it over a chair in the kitchen. "Any news from your neck of the woods?"

"I did it. I'm enrolled for next semester."

"Great news, son!" She hugged him again. "I'm proud of you."

"Yes, and I've decided to stay at Granbo's until I complete my master's. It's okay with her. We get along well, and she doesn't cramp my style."

Karen chuckled. "I'm sure she doesn't."

"So where's the painting I've been hearing about?"

Karen looked at Drew in surprise. "You know about that? Adrian just brought it last week."

"Jocelyn told me about it. Where is it?"

"It's in the family room. Come look."

Drew followed his mother down the hall. His mouth fell open when he spotted the portrait, and he stared at it for a long minute. His voice was distant when he spoke.

"Beautiful, Mom. I remember when you were like that. That look on your face, like you're just about to wink. You know, you had that same look on your face today when you rode up on the bicycle."

"Did I really?" Karen sounded pleased. "That's good because I intend to have that look more often." She paused, remembering.

A look of pure joy on your face, a wink in your eye.

Karen continued. "Furthermore, I want you to have that look on your face too, Drew."

He colored slightly. "What about Jocelyn? No look for her?"

Karen grinned. "Oh, I don't think she needs any coaching."

Drew studied the picture again. "I don't know what my face actually looks like, but I feel like I have that look when I'm sailing. I had an absolute blast on Mr. Van Gilder's boat. The harder the wind blew, the more exhilarated I felt. The rougher the seas, the more I enjoyed it. I loved the feeling of the salt air in my face. And when the boat was heeled over until the mast was almost parallel to the ocean—that's the part I liked the best."

Karen could see the passion in Drew's face as he spoke. "Wow, I'm impressed. Who knows, maybe you have some sailor blood in you from your Finnish ancestors."

Drew shrugged. "Maybe so. Anyway, Mr. Van Gilder told me about some classes I can take, and he said they always need extra crew for races at his sailing club. He said I could crew for him in a race week after next."

Karen felt a tingle of excitement for her son. "How exciting! I'm so glad you met Mr. Van Gilder. Does he remind you of your dad at all?"

Drew shook his head. "No. Dad was much more sensitive and a better listener. Mr. Van Gilder is an enthusiastic sailor, but he kind of orders people around."

"That definitely does not sound like your dad. Ari was an avid sportsman but never pushed either you or Jocelyn. Or me. He always wanted people to make decisions on their own."

Drew sighed. "I guess you're right. I always wanted to please Dad though even if he didn't push."

Sensing a slight despondency in her son, Karen decided to move on. "And how about Grace? Are you dating?"

"Hold on, Mom!" Drew chuckled. "Are you anxious to get me married off or something?"

"No," she said, grinning. "I'm just curious. You know me."

Drew smiled sheepishly. "We're pretty low-key right now, both working on our own issues, but we enjoy each other's company. We take walks, go for coffee. Stuff like that."

Karen took in a deep breath then exhaled. "Ah, youth. Always lots of time. That reminds me, did I tell you? I've invited Lisa to come home with Jocelyn for Labor Day."

Drew shook his head in amazement. "Yes, I'd like to meet Lisa. I haven't had that chance yet."

"Would you like to invite Grace as well?" asked Karen.

Drew looked thoughtful. "Nice idea, Mom, but I don't think we're ready for that yet. Besides, I imagine her family has big plans. They usually do."

"Well, if you decide at the last minute you'd like to bring her, don't hesitate. It will be fine with me. I am really looking forward to the return of our family dinners."

"You know, Mom, it's so great that we can talk about things now. Especially about Dad." He paused then went on. "Don't think I'm crazy, but sometimes I think I hear Dad speaking to me, giving me advice."

Karen's eyes teared. "I know, Drew. Sometimes I do too. Sit down." She patted the space next to her on the sofa, thinking of Ari's words: *But Drew could have used my help.*

Drew smiled and sat next to her.

"So is it good advice you hear from your father?" Karen asked.

"Yup, you bet."

CHAPTER 61

D rew was pleased that Granbo offered to take him to the Hartford train station Friday evening so that he wouldn't have to leave his Mustang in long-term parking for the weekend. Dressed in his new blue-and-green barber-striped cotton shirt and stone-colored khakis, he was excited about visiting Jocelyn for the first time since last winter.

"Have a good time in the city, dear, and give that sister of yours a hug for me. Tell her I'm really looking forward to seeing her on Labor Day."

"Thanks, Granbo. I'll tell her. See you at 5:35 Sunday night. Hope you have a good weekend."

"Oh, it will be busy, dear. Lots of clients, including Roseanne Van Gilder." Helen gave Drew a playful, teasing wink. "I'll be here Sunday night. If you're going to be late, just let me know."

On the train, Drew found a comfortable seat and reached into his backpack for his sketchbook to help pass the time. He was working on a picture of Igor from a photograph he'd taken a couple of summers ago.

Drew felt very bad about the recent mishap with Igor and kept hoping that Igor would be found. He planned to give the sketch to the Wilsons when he finished it if they wanted it.

"Penn Station!" the conductor called out. Drew was astonished. The time had literally flown by. But then he always seemed to lose track of time when he sketched. He stuffed his sketchbook into his backpack and scrambled off the train. He had planned to take a taxi to the family apartment, as he usually did, but to his surprise, Jocelyn was waiting for him at the top of the escalator in her usual faded jeans and an attractive pale aqua V-neck T-shirt.

"Drew, over here," she called out. She gave him a quick hug then stepped back to study his face.

"Hey, Josey, what's up?" Drew asked, wondering why his sister stared at him.

"You're so tan," Jocelyn exclaimed. "You look like you've just returned from the Caribbean. I've always thought of you as a paleface, you know, in the house all the time reading books, drawing."

Drew chuckled. "That's kind of how I feel too," he said as they walked toward the station exit. "I haven't been to the Caribbean, but I've spent every weekend this summer working as crew on someone's sailboat in a race somewhere. Grace's dad got me started, and I love it. I don't even need to own a boat, his club is always looking for someone to crew."

"That's great, Drew." Jocelyn began to walk down the street as they spoke, and Drew automatically kept pace with her. "I thought you might be hungry and that we could get a bite to eat before we go to the apartment. Would that suit you?"

"Sounds good, sis. I hadn't thought about it. I was busy on the train, but now that you mention it, I am hungry."

"Busy on the train? What were you doing?"

He shrugged. "Just drawing. I'll show you later."

"Okay, it's a deal. It's early, so I didn't figure we'd really need a reservation. One of my favorite places to eat in this area is the Captain's Grill. Only three blocks from here. They have great steaks, and it's inexpensive. Does this sound good?"

"I could go for a good steak right now. Let's do it."

After they were seated in the restaurant, Jocelyn ordered a filet mignon with baked potato, and Drew ordered a rib eye with french fries and onion rings.

They chatted as they sipped their soft drinks and waited for their food.

"Getting back to your sailing, Drew, I remember now that you were going to take some lessons."

"Yup. I've read all the books, passed all the written tests so far, and had lots of opportunity to just get out there and sail."

"That's terrific," said Jocelyn, the corners of her eyes crinkled as her smile widened. "I'm so pleased for you."

"Yup," Drew continued, his voice thick with amazement. "There's just something about the feel of the wind in your face and the smell of the salt air. It's so freeing." He inhaled deeply through his nose then closed his eyes and exhaled, a smile on his lips.

"Sounds therapeutic," said Jocelyn.

"Definitely," said Drew, opening his eyes. "I still see Dr. Manley though." He chuckled. "What a guy. Always wearing those flowery shirts. Doesn't give a damn what anybody thinks. Blurts out his bizarre statements. But such a big heart, and he makes me laugh."

"Amazing," said Jocelyn. "I remember when you were in the hospital you didn't seem very impressed with him. In fact, I got the impression he pissed you off."

"True enough, Josey. But what can I say? Things change."

"No kidding," said Jocelyn, thinking back to the young man who had come to visit her in this same apartment last March. *Was that really only five months ago?*

Their food arrived, and they both dove into their plates.

"Obviously, we were both hungry for steak," said Drew. "This is one of the best I've had, almost as good as the ones Dad used to cook on the grill."

"I'll second that. This is my favorite steak place at the moment. Actually, Adrian was the one who told me about it. He and I came here once, and I've been back a few times since."

Drew raised an eyebrow. "How often do you see Adrian?"

"We walk sometimes. We've golfed twice this summer. Once in a while, we meet for lunch."

"You know, Josey, I think I'm ready to talk to him now. I'm actually envious of your relationship with him. I'd like to get to know the man that Dad loved too. I couldn't do it before, but I want to now."

"Adrian was very worried about you when you were in the hospital and afterwards. He asked me every few days how you were doing. I'm sure he'd like to see you. I'll call him after we get home if you'd like."

*   *   *

Jocelyn opened the door to the apartment, and they both walked in.

Drew glanced around at the familiar surroundings. "It's nice to be back in this apartment again, Josey. It feels kind of like home."

"I know, I know. I am lucky in so many ways. To have this apartment. Mom's apartment. And if it weren't for the trust, I wouldn't be able to go to paramedic school. So much seems to be falling into place right now. I'm just keeping my fingers crossed."

"Yes, you're right. I'm grateful for the trust for the same reason."

Drew tossed his backpack on the burgundy brocade sofa and sprawled out beside it. Jocelyn took a seat in the matching color velvet armchair.

"Drew, did you ever worry that you were gay like Dad?"

A puzzled grin spread over Drew's face. "Where did that question come from?" Drew said, laughing. "No, I never thought I was gay, but I was angry that he screwed up my life."

"Are you angry with me, Drew? Because of Lisa?"

"No, of course not. And I'm not mad at Dad anymore either."

"Good, then you are ready to talk with Adrian. I'll give him a call right now."

Before he could even think about stopping her, Jocelyn tapped out the number.

"Hi, Adrian. It's me. Yes, he's here. Hey, can we all get together tomorrow? Drew wants to. Your place? Well, sure. Eleven is good. Okay, I'll ask Lisa. She was coming over here anyway, so I'm sure it'll be okay. Anything I can bring? Okay, great. See you tomorrow. Thanks, Adrian. Bye."

Jocelyn placed the phone down and turned toward Drew. "Tomorrow. For brunch. You, me, and Lisa. Adrian's a great cook, and I know we're in for a treat."

"Really," said Drew. "Well, it should be interesting." He shook his head. "You sure don't waste any time considering, do you?"

"Never have, bro," Jocelyn said. "Say, what about Grace, Drew? What's happening there?"

"Oh, we're taking it slow, not rushing into anything. I think we both learned some lessons in AA, and neither of us is ready for more right now. How about Lisa? How's your relationship going?"

"Well, I'm a little confused. Not sure about things right now. Lisa wants us to live together, but I'm trying to concentrate on my EMT training right now, so I don't think that's a good idea. We have good times though. We like the same kinds of foods, same movies, and sometimes we find ourselves finishing each other's sentences."

At that moment, the telephone rang, interrupting their conversation.

"Hello?" ventured Jocelyn. She smiled at the response. "Hi, Mike. Thought you were working tonight. What's up?"

She listened for a few moments then replied, "Oh no, sorry. I'm tied up this weekend, but maybe during the week. I thought I told you already."

Jocelyn listened again then chuckled. "That's okay, I forget things too. No problem. See you next week."

She hung up the phone and turned to Drew in explanation. "I work with this guy named Mike. He makes me laugh. And sometimes we jog together after work. I told him I was tied up this weekend, but he forgot."

Before Drew could reply, Jocelyn rapped herself lightly on the forehead and said, "Omigosh, speaking of forgetting, how could I forget to tell you? Mom telephoned just before I picked you up tonight. Igor's home!"

Drew punched his arms overhead like an athlete who had just won a gold medal. "Yes!" he shouted in total jubilation.

"Yes, isn't it wonderful? Late last night, the Wilsons were about to go to bed. Mrs. Wilson thought she heard purring outside the bedroom window. She thought it couldn't be, but it was. She went to the back porch, and there was Igor, coming through his cat door! He found his way home."

"That cat has so many lives. Amazing. Oh, you wanted to know what I was drawing on the train? Well, it was Igor." Drew dug into his backpack and pulled out his sketchbook. "Here," he said, tossing it toward her.

"Sheesh, glad I'm a good catch," said Jocelyn, successfully grasping it before it hit the floor. She began to thumb through the pages. "Wow, you've really been sketching a lot again."

"Yup, I have. Look at my last sketch first. That's Igor."

"Oh yes, it is. Amazing. This is a wonderful likeness, Drew."

Jocelyn went to the first page of the sketchbook and began to go through it in order. "Look at these sailboats. Drew, you're very good at drawing ocean waves." She turned the page. "Oooh, who's this pretty woman with those soulful brown eyes?"

Drew's eyes sparkled. "Oh, that's Grace."

Jocelyn looked up from the sketchbook. "She's very attractive, Drew." A puzzled look crossed her face as she returned her gaze to the drawing. "I don't think I remember you sketching a person before. Am I right? You used to do lots of animals."

"Yup, that's true. Decided to try my hand at it after seeing that portrait of Mom. I have discovered that I like drawing people, actually. Easier than you might think. There's more in there too. You'll see."

"Hey!" said Jocelyn as she turned another page. "This is me! Cool."

Drew chuckled again. "Sure is. Glad you could recognize yourself."

Jocelyn shook her head. "Well, it's not too hard. You are very good, Drew."

"Thanks."

*   *   *

Lisa arrived at Jocelyn's apartment at ten o'clock and was introduced to Drew for the first time. The three of them chatted while drinking coffee for the next half hour then proceeded to walk the fourteen blocks north to Adrian's, talking and laughing all the way. They made a brief stop to buy a bouquet of sunflowers and multicolored gladiolas from a local gourmet market and arrived at Adrian's apartment building right on time. The doorman had been alerted to their expected visit and directed them through the ornate marble and gold lobby to the mirrored elevator. They got off on the fourth floor.

"You're going to be blown away by Adrian's place," said Jocelyn as she knocked on the door.

"Good morning," said Adrian, a warm smile lighting up his face. "Welcome, and come on in." He stood back to allow them to enter the mosaic marble foyer.

"Mmmmm, something smells good," said Jocelyn as she handed Adrian the bouquet and gave him a hug.

Adrian smiled. "Ah yes, the frittata is in the oven." He turned toward Drew. "And you must be—"

"Oh, I'm sorry," Jocelyn interrupted. "Adrian, this is Drew. Drew, Adrian."

Adrian extended his hand to Drew. "Hi, Drew, I'm so glad you're here. I've wanted to meet you for a long time."

"Good to meet you too, Adrian. Jocelyn has told me a lot about you."

"And, Lisa, good to see you again too," Adrian said, giving her a kiss on the cheek. "Why don't you all sit down here a moment," he said as he walked into the spacious living room, motioning them to sit on the warm caramel-colored leather furniture. "Excuse me while I find a vase for these beautiful flowers."

Drew took a seat in an armchair and looked around the room. The walls were painted a deep forest green and trimmed in white. The two elegant french windows at the end of the room were draped with sheer green and mango-colored window scarves. Several large potted plants stood on the floor around the room. He also noted the three modern paintings featured one of the walls, subtly and spaciously arranged all at the same level.

"What a lovely apartment," Drew murmured.

"Yes, it is," agreed Jocelyn from the sofa where she and Lisa had chosen to sit. "It's about the same age as our apartment, but the original art-deco style has been revived with contemporary touches. It has many of the original features from the '30s, like the crown molding and built-in cabinetry and the fireplace mantel."

"Before we leave, you should ask for a tour, Drew," said Lisa. "I know Adrian wouldn't mind."

Adrian returned to the living room. "The flowers are beautiful. I set them in a vase on the dining room table so we all can enjoy them while we eat. Meanwhile, how about a drink to start with? I've made up a pitcher of Tropical Frappes—that's a drink with passion fruit juice, coconut milk, banana, and pineapple. I also have coffee or mineral water or soda."

"Oh, I'll have a frappe, Adrian. Sounds delicious!" said Jocelyn.

Lisa and Drew agreed. Adrian left the room again and returned in a few minutes with the drinks and a pitcher on a tray. The tall thin glasses and the pitcher looked like they were hand painted, and each drink was decorated with an orchid and a sprig of mint.

"Aha," said Jocelyn. "I see you've been pruning your orchids!"

Adrian chuckled. "True, I do have many varieties producing at the moment."

"You grow orchids?" Drew asked.

"Yes. It's one of my hobbies. Most of them are in the dining room. Come see them," he said, rising to his feet. "And would you like to see the rest of my apartment while we have a moment, Drew? Bring your drink along, and I'll show you."

Adrian led Drew first to the dining room where half the walls continued with the same deep forest green theme of the living room, and the other half were painted a mango color. Natural light entered the room from another white-trimmed french window. Striking contemporary paintings graced the walls of this room as well, and there were at least nine large orchid plants.

"These are hard to grow, aren't they?" asked Drew.

"They're a little fussy, all right," Adrian conceded. "The light and the temperature have to be just right, and they have to be misted twice a day. I don't find it too much trouble though, and I do enjoy them."

"Yes, they're lovely," Drew agreed. "Mom would love these. Oh!" He stopped, realizing what he had just said.

Adrian was unperturbed. "Yes," he said, moving on to the kitchen. "Your mother is a talented gardener, especially with her roses. I'll bet she'd do well with orchids too. Now, here's the kitchen. I remodeled it three years ago, replacing the old enamel appliances with stainless steel, redid the cabinets in beech wood, and replaced the old countertops with granite, had the walls painted red."

"Very nice. I especially like the center island," said Drew, "and the computer station in the corner."

Next, they moved on to the two bedrooms. The guest room again had the forest green walls, but they were accented with a spirited lavender hue, inspired by a large Georgia O'Keeffe print that hung over the bed. The master bedroom walls were painted in the mango color and complimented with green, purple, and deep pink accents.

Drew could not help but notice the many pictures of his dad in the master bedroom. Although he did not comment, he was surprised at the warm feeling it gave him to see that this man had cared so deeply for his dad.

"I've never seen such a beautiful apartment, Adrian, and what views too," said Drew. "How long have you lived here?"

"About twelve years. I like the area. And I love being able to see Central Park from my window to see the changes that take place in the different seasons."

A timer began to beep in the kitchen, signaling Adrian to finish his kitchen preparations and bring the food from the warming oven to the dining room table. The sweet Italian sausage frittata just removed from the oven was accompanied by a four-cheese vegetarian pizza; a warm chicken salad with red peppers and mushrooms over spinach greens; and french toast stuffed with apples, cream cheese, and raisins.

"Wow," said Jocelyn. "You must have been up since dawn fixing this stuff!"

"No, not quite," said Adrian with a grin. "But I'm glad you called early enough last night that I could run out to the market."

"You're definitely a gourmet chef," said Lisa.

"Oh, thanks," said Adrian. "Another of my hobbies. It's a pleasure to cook for my friends. Say, Drew, your sister tells me you are continuing with school in fall, that you've decided to become a research analyst."

"That's true. I finally decided that following Dad's path and becoming a stockbroker wasn't for me. I don't have the sales personality, but being an analyst is something that appeals to me."

"You must feel good about having a goal, Drew." Adrian turned toward Jocelyn and Lisa. "I think you'll make a great EMT, Jocelyn. And Lisa, how about you? Did you always have a clear idea what you wanted to do?"

"Yes, in fact, I did. I worked with a physical therapist when I was in high school after I wrecked my leg playing softball one summer." Lisa smiled. "Actually, as I look back on it now, I think I kind of fell in love with her. But after that, I knew that's what I wanted to be. I lucked out after I graduated last January and was offered a great job at the hospital."

"You're lucky, Lisa. I was pretty much the same way. I've always enjoyed interacting with people, and I always knew I wanted to work either in television or radio. It wasn't easy, but eventually I ended up where I am today with NPR. I still love my job."

"I know Dad always loved his job too," said Drew. "For a long time, I thought that's what I should do too because he was so successful. I wanted him to be proud of me."

"He was proud of you," said Adrian. "I'm sure he would approve of your decision to become an analyst too. On another note, what have you been up to this summer?"

"Well, I've been doing quite a bit of sailing. I met a girl, you know. It's been fun. I've also done a lot of drawing. Sketching of things in nature, boat scenes, animals, and recently people. Actually I started trying to draw people after I saw the painting Dad had done of Mother."

"Ah yes, that was quite a painting. Your dad loved that artist and was delighted that he was able to commission him to do that painting. Ari loved good art, and I'm sorry he never got to see the completed work."

Jocelyn spoke up, "Well, thinking of art, you're definitely surrounded with it here. I love this painting of the beach party scene and that painting of the dancers over there too."

"Ah, Jocelyn, the beach party scene was painted by Jackson Nederby, the same artist who painted your mother. Actually I met him when I did an interview with him five years ago. Oh, and how is your mother doing?"

"I think she's enjoying her summer. We're getting along. She seems happier."

"I'm glad. Drew, I'd love to see some of your sketches sometime if I could. I've always admired people who could draw. I enjoy art, but I have never done any drawing or painting myself."

Before Drew could answer, Jocelyn spoke out, "He's good, Adrian. He's really good. He brought his sketchbook with him, and I looked through it last night."

And Lisa interjected, "It's true. I took a look at it this morning before we walked here. I think Drew is very talented."

Drew grinned at Lisa. "Thanks." He glanced around the table. "I don't mind having a fan club at all. Nope, not at all."

*   *   *

After a sumptuous mango trifle dessert and more conversation, Drew, Jocelyn, and Lisa left Adrian's apartment around three in the afternoon. They strolled through the zoo in Central Park for a while and then went to an early showing of *The Matrix* before returning to the Antilla apartment. At nine o'clock, Lisa departed for her own apartment so that she would have time to get ready for her early morning shift. Jocelyn and Drew lounged in their usual spots in the living room, feet on the coffee table.

"Nice day, sis," said Drew. "I really like Lisa, and Adrian is a totally fascinating guy."

"Yeah, he's pretty famous in the city too," said Jocelyn. "Lot's of people know who he is, from his radio broadcasts. Have you ever listened to one?"

"Nope, I haven't. Never occurred to me, but I think I will."

"Yeah, you know he even did a series on the straight spouses of gay people, from the point of view of the straight person. I think he did that with Mom in mind, wanting to help people like her."

"Really? Do you think she heard it?"

Jocelyn shook her head. "I have no idea. The subject doesn't come up with us."

Drew chuckled. "Maybe I'll bring it up then."

Jocelyn tossed a cushion at him. "Yeah, sure! Like you'd ever bring something like that up to Mom."

Drew tossed it back. "Well, why not? I'm going to make a point of telling her we met with Adrian today. The first chance I get."

Jocelyn's face scrunched into a disbelieving look. "Why?"

"Well, why not? Keeping secrets never helps anyone. For instance, let's take you and Adrian. If you'd have told her right away that you were seeing him, don't you think she would have adjusted to the idea sooner?"

"The only thing I know is that she's more accepting now than she was. But you know, I think you're right. At first when she found out about Lisa, she wanted no part of her. Now, she's come to town to take us out to lunch, and she wants her to come home with me for Labor Day. I never thought she'd change, but she did."

"Josey, we've just got to be honest. That will help Mom and us, more than anything. That's one of the things I've learned in therapy and from Grace as well."

"I wonder how Mom will feel about both of us being friends with Adrian."

Drew sighed. "I don't know. I doubt she will ever welcome him with open arms, but she may develop some respect for him. I hope. He's a nice guy. I can picture him and Dad together, and I even see some similarities between Adrian and Mom."

Jocelyn chuckled. "Yes, I know what you mean. The love of gardening and cooking and artwork. And even love of the dance."

Chapter 62

"Drew, can you help me put the food on the table? We're almost ready to eat." Karen called from the kitchen so those sitting in the family room could hear.

"Sure, I'll help," Drew said as he rose. He walked into the kitchen where his mother was surrounded by a platter of roast beef and serving dishes filled with mounds of garlic, mashed potatoes, and oven-roasted vegetables. "I'm starved. Absolutely famished."

"Good. Jocelyn, why don't you open the sparkling cider, and, Helen, would you mind pouring the ice water?"

This Labor Day celebration marked the first time the family had been together for a dinner with Helen since Ari died.

Drew carried the serving dishes to the dining room. From the time he was a young boy, he'd been the one to help his mother with dinner preparations. Jocelyn always managed to be busy with something until the last minute before a meal.

"All right, everyone. Find a spot at the table. Wherever you'd like."

Jocelyn was first to walk to the table. "Well, Mom should sit at the head of the table as she always has. I'll sit here." She took a seat on the side.

Drew hung back. Karen sensed he was reluctant to sit in his father's chair, but before she could speak, Helen chose the chair at the opposite end of the table from Karen.

"This chair suits me. I hope no one minds. Drew, I guess you'll sit there," she said, pointing to the remaining chair.

Drew exhaled noticeably as he pulled his chair out from the table.

Karen was the last to sit. "I'd like to say something before we eat." She paused, and everyone looked in her direction. "I'm glad we're together today. We've been through a lot, not only in the past few months, but in the past few years. Each of us in our own way. It's appropriate for all of us who were special to Ari to be together."

"Well, almost all of us," said Jocelyn.

Karen tried not to, but she just had to laugh. "You just couldn't help yourself, could you, dear?"

Jocelyn looked guilty. "No, I guess not, Mom. Sorry."

"It's okay. All of us are here who should be. Maybe next year. He could bring along his mango trifle for dessert."

Jocelyn and Drew burst into laughter. Helen rolled her eyes in mock disgust. "I can't believe this. I'm the only one in the family who hasn't met him other than at the hospital, for heaven's sake, and I'm the one who stuck up for him from the beginning!"

"Dad must be rolling over in his grave, listening to this discussion," said Jocelyn.

Drew spoke up. "Maybe you'll think I'm crazy, but I feel as if Dad is here too. Right in this room."

Karen looked at the painting on the wall of the adjoining family room then at Drew and smiled.

"I don't think you're crazy." Addressing everyone she said, "Shall we start? We don't want the food to get cold."

"Just a moment," said Helen. "I have some astonishing news. Yesterday, I got a phone call from Annika."

Three jaws dropped.

"Aunt Annika," blurted out Jocelyn, "I thought she was dead! We haven't heard from her since before Dad died!"

"Thank God," said Drew. "I've always prayed she would return."

Karen shook her head. "That was one of the hardest things about Ari's illness and death. That his sister didn't know because we had no idea where she was. How is she?"

"I guess she's okay," said Helen. "She's finally ready to get some help. She's in San Francisco and will be flying back next Friday to enter a treatment center."

"How did she handle the news of Ari's death?" asked Karen.

"She already knew," responded Helen. "She called Ari's office about six months after he died and pretended to be a client. They gave her the news, and apparently it really threw her into a tailspin, and I think she hit bottom. She told me she's been having dreams about her brother, and that has something to do with why she's coming home."

A look passed between Drew and Karen.

After a moment of silence, Karen spoke. "This is great news, Helen, for all of us."

The dinner continued smoothly. Karen relaxed listening to the easy chatter around her. Drew spoke of his recent sailing adventures, Helen shared stories from the salon, and Jocelyn explained the rigors of her new career.

Halfway through the meal, Karen remarked, "Too bad Lisa couldn't make it. I'd looked forward to seeing her again."

"Yes," said Helen. "I'd like to meet her too. You'll have to bring her along when you come for a haircut."

Jocelyn looked uncomfortable. "Sure, Granbo. Maybe I can do that sometime. But I don't know, we're uh . . . kind of not seeing each other right now."

"What?" Karen's fork clattered to the floor as she reached for her napkin. "You mean you broke up?"

"Well, I don't know if it's permanent or not. Right now, we're taking a hiatus."

Karen bent to pick up her fork. "Did you have a fight?"

"Not exactly. Here, let me get you a new fork." Jocelyn jumped to her feet, seized the offending fork, and disappeared into the kitchen.

She obviously doesn't want to talk about this, Karen thought to herself. *Probably hopes we'll start talking about something else while she's gone.* Momentarily, Karen considered dropping the subject but found she could not.

When Jocelyn returned, she started again. "Well, what happened, Jocelyn? I liked Lisa. I hope you can work it out."

Drew began to laugh. "I can't believe this! Just a few months ago, Mom, you were shocked at the idea of Jocelyn bringing a woman home, and now you're upset because she's not!"

Karen gave Drew a pointed look. "You can't go by first reactions, especially when the news is a shock." She paused to grin at Drew. "I reserve the right to change my mind. Always."

At that, Helen, in the middle of taking a sip of sparkling cider, choked. Everyone at the table laughed, including Karen.

Not one to be sidetracked, Karen persisted. "But you still haven't told us what happened, Jocelyn."

"Okay, Mom, I'll tell you. But the truth is, I don't understand what's going on myself. All my life, I've been attracted to women, right? Well, okay, so you didn't know, but I did. Never, not even once, did I ever have a crush on a boy. I always knew, as soon as I was old enough to understand, that I was a lesbian. And, I *still* think I am."

A puzzled look came over Karen's face. "Has there been some challenge to that?"

Again, Jocelyn squirmed. "Yes, and no. Remember, I mentioned my coworker Mike? The one who started training at the same time as me?"

Karen thought a moment. "Oh, yes, the comedian."

"That's right. Lisa always said Mike was interested in me, and I always laughed about it. But last week Mike asked me out, and I told Lisa."

Helen spoke on the subject for the first time. "Well, so what if he asked you out? That shouldn't upset her. Doesn't mean anything, except that Mike made a mistake. Right?"

Jocelyn rolled her eyes. "Wrong, Granbo. Damn, why am I cursed with this need to tell the truth? I don't know how to say this. Even though I'm convinced I'm a lesbian, Mike asked me out, and I'm interested. I don't know why, but I am, and Lisa doesn't understand it. I don't either. It just is."

Helen frowned. "I've known a couple of women through the salon who have changed their minds about their sexual orientation several times over the course of their lives."

"Josey," said Drew, "whatever you are, it's fine with me, as long as you're happy."

Karen leaned back in her chair, raised her eyebrows, and let out a big sigh as she looked heavenward for a moment. Karen could not help but think of Ari and the struggle he must have felt. *Tortured* was the word Adrian had used. She wondered why it was so easy now to empathize with her daughter when she had been unable to do so with Ari. At least, until just now.

She began to speak, slowly and quietly. "Drew's right. The only place the answers come from, Jocelyn, is within."

* * *

The leftovers were tucked in the refrigerator, the dishwasher had been loaded, unloaded, and the dishes put away; and Jocelyn was asleep in her bedroom upstairs. Helen and Drew had left more than two hours ago. Now it was time to put her feet up.

Karen poured a glass of wine and headed for her recliner. She kicked off her shoes, settled into the chair, and leaned back. The evening was over, and it had been a success. She and Helen had even managed to get along although it had taken some effort. Just the same, she was glad to have Helen as part of the family dinner table again. She'd missed her and her colorful stories. And now the news about Annika, returning to the fold at last. Karen hoped her recovery program would work.

Thinking of recovery, Drew was coming along well. Karen could see it was still difficult for him to speak up, but more and more he was voicing his opinions.

And Jocelyn. As strong as she always presented herself, she was still on the path of finding her own way. Her daughter had just discovered she was not quite as together as she had imagined. At least she was enjoying her job.

Karen sighed and swirled the wine around in the glass. She wished she could say the same. Of course, she did still enjoy teaching the kids. It was the administrative business and paperwork that were so frustrating, but she supposed that was present in many jobs. She did have to admit that school matters hadn't weighed so heavily on her lately. Having other things to do, like biking, lightened the load. Maybe she should get involved with some other activities as well.

She glanced at her picture on the wall. Like dancing. Maybe she should go to a class. She'd have to check into that. Maybe Melissa would want to go too. That was another thing she was enjoying, having a friend to do things with.

She placed her half-empty glass on the small table next to her then leaned back and closed her eyes. Soon she realized she was in a half-awake, half-dream state, and her eyes flew open. The last time she'd felt like this . . . she looked cautiously around the room. No one. She didn't know whether to be happy or sad.

Then it dawned on her. There had been no more appearances of Ari since . . . since that conversation in the bedroom. Oh, sure, she'd thought of things he said. But she didn't see him. She didn't hear him. The thoughts were . . . her own.

She looked toward the picture window, and in the night reflection, she could see herself sitting in her recliner. She looked peaceful. And happy. And alive. In fact, she looked like . . .

Karen turned away from the reflected image and studied the portrait. She remembered his words.

Hush, beautiful . . . you can tell me good-bye when you see yourself as I picture you . . . That will be the time.

Slowly, she sat up and reached for her glass. Raising it to the portrait, she whispered,

"Good-bye, Ari. And thank you." She took a long swallow and looked back at the window, just in time to see Igor stroll by, his tail rising like a plume of smoke.